Preppers Road March

RON FOSTER

ISBN-13:
978-1466225398

ISBN-10:
1466225394

Acknowledgment

To My Special Friend Cheryl Chamlies For All Her Inspiration and Support

1

Grid Down

Ah hell! David muttered to himself as he began trying to look around the room after the lights went out in the restaurant just minutes after sitting down and receiving his menu.

"Hey Jack?" He inquired of the shadow sitting next to him, "Have you been having brown outs in the city lately?"

"Not that I know of" Jack responded. "But Atlanta always has some kind of shortage of infrastructure capacity and common sense going on" he grumbled. Jack was going to be David's new boss at FEMA and after he had just passed the final interview process this morning, Jack was welcoming his new Emergency Planner to the area by buying lunch for him and bringing along the areas section chief for an introduction.

Blake the area's section chief was a grizzled old First Sergeant from the Vietnam era that had retired from the Army and was soon to retire from his second career at FEMA. Me and Blake I decided, were going to get along just fine, as it was he who had suggested this particular restaurant with a sly wink towards my direction, that this place was his hangout and part of his way he of getting to know folks in his command at the familiar environs of the bar attached to it, and "Helloooooo! Do you like beer or whiskey as your poison of choice?" Blake asked me.

"Don't need to ask me twice to help indulge in some adult beverages, but I best explain." I told him, "I have a bit of Native American in me and although I love the whiskey, it doesn't love me." The last statement produced a loud guffaw from the old bar reveler.

"David, you are all right! You know your limitations." Blake did look at me a bit comically evil and said, "I might test your limits later though with some good sour mash whiskey."

"That would be Jack and Coke for me." I replied. But I protested to my new leader, "Hey, you're supposed to lead me away from my downfalls, not towards them." I say with a chuckle.

He looked serious about this for a moment and said, "I need to see you at your worst, so I know if you will restrain yourself at your worst, while still trying to do your best."

Well, that's one subject I am not going there on, so I tried to direct the conversation to something else that showed my experience with alcohol, without any admissions to my possibly wavering ways or occasional wilder side tendencies, that I learned the hard way to curb. He started eying my shoes and made some comment about needing a little touch up polish.

Damn, I thought, this old goomer who had been pushing troops his whole life should lighten up on the personal quizzing and inspection, he already knows every trick and excuse, but we aren't in 'this Man's Army': as I say, "no more" and his scrutiny down to a 'boot inspection' is not something a old seasoned trooper should have to endure. For those of you readers not familiar with the era of the last military basic training cycles of "Nam" requiring a "boot inspection". It is a degrading and necessary adaptation to military life that is at first experienced by those uninitiated soon after the point when you sign that first bit of paper that that swears your allegiance to America and the Constitution and that resolutely puts you in the Army for the duration of your enlistment.

Everybody joins the military for their own reasons. I can summarize based on my own experience why anyone would do it now and join up for the same economic hardships we faced then. A statement by one of my former Drill sergeants regarding enlistments can be summarized as a quote. The number one understanding to relate to all reasons people enlist is 'A bare ass, bare pockets and a bare cupboard, will put you in the military'. I did it myself and remain proud that I signed on the dotted line, because I was a dumbass first and foremost to the facts of real war, ignorant to the facts of life and also needed the ultimate way out of my then current situation, as so many others choose to do.

But, I digress, the reader really wants to know at this point what's up with the analogy of the "marked boots" thingy I mentioned. When you're sorry trainee ass arrived at boot camp in my day (hippie era early 70s), you get eventually herded into a warehouse to get your 'basic issue' in every branch of service. You get measured and rushed down a dizzying array of equipment and a line of folks throwing gear at you, that you put into one of two duffel bags. One is for field equipment; one is personal clothes under the ID of uniforms, including your civvies you walked in with. When you go out the door, if you're a man, your head has been shaved to make everyone appear uniform and you can't recognize anybody after that, including yourself, and now you are also carrying two 40 plus inch canvas or nylon bags approximately 65lb to 75 lb each of BS, that is your gear and goods needed for this new career to account for as well as the papers assigning it to you.

3

At sometime in this process of being herded about, you are told to grab one pair of your two pair of boots and put them on your feet that have been covered with your civilian shoes up to this point. Then you are told to step up on a wooden stool, face front and allow someone to take a pencil eraser they dip in white gummy paint to apply it to the top of the boots you are now wearing. I wore black boots then you had to polish, just keep in mind times are changed now. One dot per boot for two reasons, you are too dumb to remember to change your boots every other day for hygiene purposes and so the DI can get on your ass, if you forget or try to cheat. I included this bit of reminiscing for those that think about signing up for the most eye-opening experience that you will ever have, put some dots on your daily wear shoes and then try to explain them to friends without my ramble, you can't do it unless …. Seen it, done it been there.

Let us get back up to the here and now, as some folks might say. After a moment or two of the restaurant's elevator music being shutdown by the power outage, the normally subdued voices of the restaurants patrons began to murmur loudly and inquisitively about what to do next. The normally helpful and subdued waiters and waitresses began to lose their cool amongst what was starting to look like a laser light show of little flashlights flipping back and forth across the room, as they turned to respond to the next dufus customer loudly grousing about if the power would be back on soon, 'I don't think I should have to pay for this' etc.

Blake was totally unperturbed about this and said, "Let's go out to the porch bar until this shit settles," as he flicked on a little photon light on his key ring to guide the way.
Acknowledging this was the best idea we had heard all day, Jack and I made haste to follow the old First Shirt through the

maze of tables and freaked out staff. The staff at this point was retreating towards the establishments center bar to confer with the managers on what to do next, thus leaving the patrons in the dark to their dismay, when we swung open the door to a bright sunlight lit Tiki Bar looking affair on the back deck.

"What's up Sarge!?" said an old NCO club manager looking type. as he was already mixing Blake's favorite potion of a Singapore Sling.

"Powers out!" roared Blake, as he sidled up to the bar and started searching his pockets for one of those little cigars I hadn't seen in years. "David, this is our medic and bartender friend, Bob. He will also answer to a few other names that you might hear before the night wears out."

I grinned as these two old soldiers embraced and noticed that Jack wasn't having any problem getting his drink without ordering it yet either. Bob extended his hand with an exaggerated gesture and said, "So you're the latest master of disaster going to work for frick and frack," dutifully eying Jack and Blake.

"Yeah, that would be me," I admitted, then I tried to ease my way into a more comfortable conversation after enduring a painful pause of scrutiny, while watching the twinkle in his eye as a side glance went to Top. I have seen that look before, I recollected, amongst the old mud boot military cadre, it meant 'what do you really think of this recruit?' A quick nod by both my superiors, and a slap on the back by Jack, meant 'he is ok' and we settled down to enjoy our drinks, in that camaraderie all ex-service men share.

"You ever have been to Atlanta before?" asked Bob in my general direction, as he started to serve some more patrons pouring in the side door to take advantage of our great idea to partake of adult beverages in the light of day.

"Yes. I used to be a stockbroker up here awhile back," I replied.

"A 'legalized bookie,' huh!" cried Bob with a laugh. "We got several kinds of those weasels that make their home here. Hey, Bill come on and meet David." he exclaimed pointing a finger in my direction.

Bill was an Armani suit wearing, manicured, stuck up ass who I think breed in the gutters of the financial district of Bankhead and that always seem to be some sort of a inbreed Atlanta lounge lizard there. Bill half assed waved at me, and then said something about not starting any shit to the bartender, who just smirked happily back, secure in his own domain and place in the city's pecking order. The bar had crisscrossed timbers for shade and several ceiling fans lazily stirred the humidity, but it did not seem to be doing anything to help beat the 95 degree Georgia heat, so I loosened my tie and got out of my suit coat.

Jack asked me if I had a long drive this morning coming in from Montgomery, Alabama. I replied, "No, the trip was not too bad, because I missed a lot of the rush hour traffic during travel times." I reminded the group that I had a 10.00 o'clock appointment with them, so I had left out at 6.30 AM to be on the safe side and it took me about three hours to get in to town. I remarked I sure would like to see the power comeback on so I could get something to eat, because I hadn't had the opportunity to munch anything today. Bob said I would hear the cash register cycle when it did and shoved some pretzels my way to tide me over. Meantime, I see his boss and what looks to be a bouncer waving him down from the corner and he trotted off to their summons.

I told Blake I was going to the restroom, if I could find it, and would he give me navigation directions.

"You want to borrow my light, David?" he asked while waving a ham size fist full of keys it was attached too.

"No thanks." I said, "Got my own." and waved my keys back at him.

"What the hell you got on that thing?" Jack exclaimed, as he was eying what evidently he thought was some kind of huge baffling mystery of accumulated key ring add-ons.

I laughed and said, I'd explain it all when I got back. But at the moment, my back teeth were floating and I was in a hurry to recycle some of the beer that I had consumed with him and his partner's interview process.

I wandered back into the restaurant shining my light in front of me and noticed they had raised what few shades there were and that the front doors were open with quite a loud commotion of voices drifting in from outside. Lights were still out, so I didn't think bar fight or anything other than the restaurant and customers bitching about bills. I took care of my business and was headed back out the door to rejoin my comrades, but got interested in what appeared to be a mob of people at the front door of the business just milling around. I need to go be nosy; I thought and proceeded to check out what the fuss was about. As I neared the doors I heard I heard a hubbub of voices asking 'what would cause a car not to work?' and 'why are they cars stalled?' etc., I then got a sinking feeling as I exited the doors.

'Oh shit. Lord protect us!' I thought, as I see disabled cars and the drivers psycho-babbling about. Frigging EMP! Now wait, it's not nuclear caused, well as near as I can tell at the moment. Skies clear, no tell tale mushroom cloud, etc. Think man think. Ok, radiation is not a worry for the moment; maybe this is a natural event. Haven't I been repeating the warning that NASA already put out about solar storm cycles and CME events for years? Well, Merry Christmas, your ass is stuck in the middle of the hell you predicted.

7

Spread the Word

"Daaaamnn!" I was drawling out to myself in my southern fried accent, *what to do, what to do,* as I reentered the restaurant, *ok go calm David. Hey! There's a steak knife on that table, I need that and slipped it in my suit pants pocket.* It was one of those rounded point, politically correct jobs, that although I was bitching about it not having a usable point, but no... *"oat meal beats no meal'* AND! I was glad it wasn't a worry to slide in my pocket. I had a knife. I had an edge for multiple survival tasks I needed to perform soon. As I opened the door to the bar, I thought about all the years of Risk Communications I had studied, but studies didn't prepare me for what I had to do next and that steak knife in my pocket was a joke if I thought it was

the best advice I could give on how to get through the crap hitting the fan I'd just witnessed.

Jack was grinning like a Cheshire cat when I returned and said, "Ok, lemme see that key ring!"

I said, "Jack, poke Blake and come talk to me over here, I got some SITRAP to share (situation report)."

Blake was giving Bill hell about never having served in the military and objecting to Bills BS liberal, negative attitude on FEMA`s response to Katrina, when a poke to the ribs got his attention.

"WHAT!" Blake said, as he had slightly alcohol induced steely daggers coming out his eyes in our direction.

"David requires our attention to some problem and is looking awful serious." Jack said.

"Better be good." Blake hissed and followed us towards the decks railing.

Before arriving at the railing, I turned and hesitantly said, "Come over here," while lowering my voice.

"DAMMIT, Dupree!" Blake directed at me, "I don't take interference well, so what the hell is your problem needing such urgent attention?"

I stared into the big old mans eyes and said, "'Houston, we got a problem' is about all I can say that fits this."

Puzzled, he looked at me and I waved them both closer to the railing instructing both to, "Have a look."

Peachtree St., the artery to the city and the heart of the financial district, as far as the eye could see in both directions, was Kaput! Cars, trucks, service vans etc. littered the scenery as far as the eye could see. All the vehicles and occupants were in various states of disarray depending on the driving skills of the operators. People were just stopped in the streets, people were on curbs, newly attached to light poles, head on wrecks, rear ended etc. it was a Machiavellian hell. This wasn't a power outage-party anymore; it was every Emergency Management offices' worse nightmare!

Simultaneously both my bosses said, "Oh HELL!' and I responded," You got that right."
"We got to get moving," said Jack.
"Yeah, but where?" I asked Blake.
Lord help him he is a card, said "First back to our drinks and then talk privately about the bar tab." Heads turned up to eye each other, solemn nods and back to the bar we went. Jack ordered a new round to refresh the drinks we swallowed in kind immediately and then we moved off from the rest of the 40 or so revelers, who had not a clue yet as to what had just happened to end the world as we had known it.

I got to give it to Blake, after serving more than 45years for his country, he wanted to stay on duty and make it back the 13 miles by foot to the closest FEMA headquarters to try to help with this situation. Jack and I glanced at one another, considered and nothing more needed to be said. There were no plans for this type of event that we could help with, and we had family and friends to help survive. We turned to Blake to try to dissuade him, but he hushed our objections with a wave of his hand.
He said, "Look, I don't have anyone but me basically and you are the only troops I can look out for, so...let me give you 10 minutes of advice and then get your asses out of here."
"But...," I interjected.
And before I could carry on, he hammered one of those giant meat hooks some people call hands on me and said, "Hush, I got my duty. You, David, are low man on the totem pole, so you listen to me first. Go get Bob to give you two pitchers of water and three shots of Jack. Tell him the Jack Daniels is for me, he understands and will get the message."

"While David goes on a mission, I will discuss something with you, Jack, privately," he said refocusing his attention to the street out front.

Well, while I dutifully ordered up at the bar and returned to our table, I was haunted by the way Bob had looked, when I gave Blake's 'special order'. He was still his old self hurrahing the bar, but he was a changed man somehow. He'd gotten that 'thousand yard stare' those of us that seen battle get: a new determination and resolve that, well to the untested, is just plain scary. It is like dead eyes looking at you and you just know someone is about to kick your ass and they have no doubt they can do it. I turn around and glance back at Jack and Blake, and they are locked into one of those 8 inch conversations you know means business. Meantime, Bob is discussing something intensely with the bouncer named 'Dump Truck' and staring in my direction. Bob hands me my order and says to talk to 'Dump' before I leave, and then he is back in his happy bartender mode waiting on the rest of the bar, as I make my way back to the table.

3

DISPLACED PREPPER

I put the drinks and pitchers of ice water down on the table, and before I even take my seat, Blake has corralled all the shots of whiskey over to his side. "Last call trainee," he says in my direction. "This is my whiskey. I am kicking you out of the bar."

"Do what!!?" I start to object before 'the Look' silences me.

"You and Jack are going home. It's best you play camel with that water, because it's a hot day and you won't see ice water again for a long, long time, if you catch my drift."

"Where's your shit, David?" Jack asks.

"What shit?" I reply, getting aggravated at my seniors and Blake snatching 'my' whiskey shot, which I was thinking I really needed about now.

Blake chimes in with, "We already figured out you are a prepper and you rode over here with Jack. You SOL son. Yeah shit out of luck, except that monkey knot looking key ring full of doodads you got. I don't think you were dumb enough to conceal carry your pistol to the interview or into this bar, so how far away are your preps, and where are you staying?"

This is a smart man I am talking to, he is used to field soldiers having problems with life and helping them come up with a fix. Is there extra hope here? I consider why he asked before responding.

"I am about 18 miles in the opposite direction of travel, my hotel is north and I am heading south." Oh, oh, here comes that know-it-all finger wagging telling me to pause before speaking further I thought, *'Asshole you want me to call you Drill sergeant, too?'* I am sort of thinking to myself before he begins his communication and my education into his worldly outlook on things.

Blake said, "Look, Jack and I have talked about it and you got 4 options to consider. *'Hell that's news to me, I am all ears.'* First option is you can see Jack home; he has preps and will take you in. Second option is me, I am heading for the Governor's offices and you can do what you trained to do in disaster response. Third is go off with Dumpie, he is heading south, but east of your location. And the fourth and final option is for you to go do what you got to do on your own."

After a moments hesitating on the pros and cons of the choices, I proposed to take Dump Truck along as far as the journey would allow, but I was adamant about heading all 180 plus miles home to Montgomery.

What's a displaced prepper to do?

13

4

PACK MULE INCOPORTATED

I start thinking friggin bad decision to pick the Dump as a traveling companion, he has been bitching from the moment we left the bar. Yeah, he is a 380 pound monster, but he doesn't have the sense God gave a goat about some things. Now don't get me wrong there are certain advantages of wandering down the street in the middle of pandemonium with your own one man division beside you. That being said he would not shut up and let me think of what I needed to be doing next. He was naming off every appliance he could think of, wondering if they would still work when the power came back on; what he should do with them if it didn't. Which ones might hypothetically could have started a fire when they got fried? Then he started running down the list of every, half cousin and relative he had in the county, etc., and what were they doing and saying about this or that appliance no longer working.

I begin to finally like his big old country boy ass a bit better after he quieted down a bit and figured out that all his psycho babbling was his way of dealing with stress. We must have looked like a very odd pair wandering down the street and arguing like Abbott and Costello, but in the looks department we couldn't have been any different. Dump was 25 and bald with the sleeve tattoo thing going on, and I was tall and thin with the silver gray hair carrying various parts of a three piece suit. I had been inquiring of passers by all the way down the street about who sells water and other goods in this desolate (lack of convenience stores) area of Atlanta. A lot of people took one look at Dump, saw their worst nightmare was standing before them that they hadn't thought about yet, and realizing the position they were in now, actually changed sides of the road or didn't answer at all and kept moving as quickly away as they could. We changed course twice to find some kind of store with bottled water, got off the main drag, and then I see a typical tiny India Indian run store and sure enough they are open! Yee ha!

I explained to the Dump I got 50 bucks cash; he said he had 17 bucks and credit cards. "Get off asking me about credit card balances, Dumpie! Nobody will take them now anyway, and I have been hearing this same bitching about 2 miles now. I got them, you got them, we have walked pass about a hundred ATMs, they aren't going to work, not ever again or not for a long time to come! Yea I know your boss was dumb enough to cause minor riots at the restaurant and bar to charge someone on a later day by writing card numbers down and you blocked the door with your big ass and I had to wait on you, but I have been telling you for at least 3miles now this city wont recover anytime soon or it will take at least 3 months if a localized thing, or maybe never because I am not sure yet what caused the EMP." I suspected a CME though, a coronal mass ejection sort of like a giant solar flare. If that was the case then, it wasn't just the US that had a problem, the lights were out throughout the world and we were back to the 1800s as far as technology went.

PACK MULE INC.

The store was your typical office building type, about the size of newsstand with some coolers and a couple isles of snacks etc. I hadn't told Dump truck about my leather money belt I had on with a few hundred cleverly concealed inside what looked like a normal belt. I had two packs of cigs on me and was strongly considering buying a carton when I came to my senses and said now's the time to quit whether I want to or not. I am still buying one pack out of spite for the road though, my nerves are frazzled enough and I am going to enjoy my vice just for a little while longer.

The stores owner flinched as Dump blocked out the light coming in the door, but he soon affably regained his composure and began his mantra for the occasion. "Bad day, Bad day for everyone my friends, cash only, no power, cash only! You buying something today mister?" he inquired. The stores owner said all this with a thick accent and all in one breath about as fast as he could in a lilting sing song way.

"No problem" I replied. The Dump had already agreed to let me do most of the shopping so he started moving quick towards the water and me towards the can goods. Six cans of tuna cleaned out the shelf, $3 a piece (damn the prices) two cans of Vienna sausages ($4.50) some crackers and hard candies, and my $6.50 pack of cigs I met dump at the register and he had 12 bottles of water at a $1.75 a piece. We got out the door with about 3 bucks change. This stuff was way to awkward to be toting around in thin plastic bags I thought and told dump put his bags on the park bench out in front of the store and I would see about repositioning our load.

I was about to start cutting the sleeves off my jacket and rigging them up to make a sort of pack mule collar for my buddy to carry with my tie as a strap, when I spied what appeared to be a painter's van at the corner of the road.

Hang on a sec "Dump Truck" I will back in a minute. I was looking at all the people standing around or hurriedly passing by to see if anyone looked like a painter as I approached the vehicle... The catastrophe had only hit a few hours ago and the owners of the van might still be in the area. I checked the backdoors of the van and was in luck, they were unlocked. I peered inside and saw stacks of tarps. Bingo, I grabbed two of the smallest and then crawled up into the van with several fervent looks around to see if anyone was taking particular notice of my actions. I moved some buckets out of my way and saw a couple of those cheap disposable plastic painters tarps you can buy at the dollar store that are small enough to put in your back pocket and snagged them and a piece of frayed nylon rope about 10ft. long.

I popped out of the van and carried my loot back to Dump, who was looking bewildered and worried at my antics.

"What are those for David?" he inquired. "I thought you might have been coming back with a 5gallon bucket or something to tote this shit in"

"Live and learn my big friend, I am going to show you how to make a horseshoe pack out of these tarps" I replied.

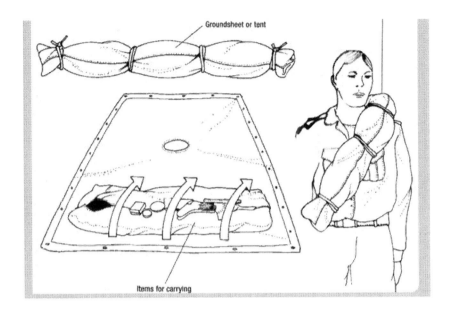

This pack is simple to make and use and relatively comfortable to carry over one shoulder. Lay available square-shaped material, such as poncho, blanket, or canvas, flat on the ground. Lay items on one edge of the material. Pad the hard items. Roll the material (with the items) toward the opposite edge and tie both ends securely. Add extra ties along the length of the bundle. You can drape the pack over one shoulder with a line connecting the two ends

I folded my coat in one of the tarps and divided up our purchases between our two packs. I thought about making him carry it all, but if something happened to him or we got separated, I needed my half of what few supplies there were. We set off back on our journey looking a bit out of place with our paint spotted packs slung around us, but we didn't care, we knew the road ahead was going to be long and the weight of some food and water no matter how we were carrying it was reassuring.

"What cha in the mood to eat Dump Truck?" I said to the puffing sweating behemoth beside me.

"What are you talking about, David?" he responded.

"We going to hit a block of restaurants in the next mile or so" I offered.

"Fat lot of good that will do us," then he hesitated. "What do you have in mind?" he said with a conspiratorial look.

"Well, the way I see it we are 5 or 6 hours into this thing. The recognition of the SHTF is now just dawning on the majority of the Sheeple, but look around the parasites are already gathering to plot and scheme some dastardly deeds".

"Yeah, I been noticing that last mile or two," said Truck. "The homeless and the gang banger types are seeming to be coming out of the wood works and just waiting for nightfall or something else to happen".

"Exactly," I responded. "Let's take a break and I will tell you my plan."

The Last Supper or Going Dumpster Diving

"You see, Dumpster" I said.

"Hey, don't call me that!" he snarled back, but actually came off looking like a hurt little schoolboy much to his chagrin.

"Ok, no problem, Dump. You see these restaurants up ahead are the ritzy type mostly and the patrons will be either gone or still having partying in the bars possibly."

"Yeah, so what? How does that help us get a meal?" he said, rubbing his noggin with a dinner plate sized hand.

"Well," I replied, "'Hard times make for hard decisions'." .I advised. "A lot of food is going to get left on plates in the restaurants part eaten."

"Oh hell no!" Dump objected.

"That's funny," I said, "You don't look like a picky eater." I poked at him.

"We got some food, we don't have to do that crap." whined Dump.

"How far is it to just get to the edge of Atlanta from here?" I asked.

He pondered for a minute, "Maybe 20-30 miles?"

I said, "Yup, and we on the close end of this place to go south. It's going to take us two or three days to just get to the first exit. Believe me, as unpalatable as snagging a half eaten steak that has been sitting on somebody's plate for a few hours sounds, we need to eat while we can easily get it."

"Steak, huh? That doesn't sound so bad now. I can deal with that." he replied.

"Speaking of night zombies, after we chow down we are going to jump the embankment down to the interstate. I don't want to get caught in the downtown area when the sun goes down."

"It already sounds like the natives are getting restless," he replied, as gunfire echoed off in the not so far distance.

"I am not so much worried about them at the moment. You notice how much more smoky and hazy it's gotten?"

Truck said, "Now that you mention it, yeah, it has and it's not that same ozone smell of the transformers blowing either."

I started scanning around said, "It's hard to see exactly what's going on in the sky from under these skyscrapers." and then I stopped mid track. Hartsfield Airport was sort of on the track we were headed and was probably a burning inferno by now.

I explained to Dump that planes would have been falling out of the sky, running into each other on the tarmac etc., just like a lot of the wrecks we saw on the road we were traveling, because of the EMP. We might be heading into a hellfire and not even know it, if enough things get to burning a phenomenon called a

21

fire wind is created and just like a forest fire, whoosh it's on you before you know it.

The Fate's sure were having fun messing up my dinner plans today. Ok, time to regroup and do a risk assessment. I told The Dump that according to my educated risk assessment the chances of that whole huge airport eventually burning to the ground were more likely than not and we needed to skirt it best we could. The highway 85 running to our right was our best route to get away from the congested downtown area, but it might not be the best choice either.

"Why is that?" Truck moaned, as the various complexities of our day were getting a bit much for him to wrap his head around.

"You know how many 18 wheelers come through the highways here? No telling what they are carrying." I replied.

"You mean possible HazMat spills?" Dump asked.

"You have been listening to Jack and Blake talking." I said with a grin.

"I do hear things you know." he informed me.

"Well, this section of the road might be ok." I said. "See, part of what I was supposed to be helping with up here, was figuring out where all the off ramps for the Hazmat carrying trucks were in relation to residential areas and beefing up the emergency plans. The DOT is real particular on what can be hauled through the city and has to go around it on the outside loop highways most of the time."

"Yeah, I have seen the 'hazardous material trucks must exit' signs on the highway," he said.

"And did you?" I replied at him with a smirk.

"Did I what?" he questioned.

"Exit." I said.

"Ok, you asshole, I get it, Ha, Ha. No, I didn't." He begrudgingly replied.

"Let's start heading off to the right down one of these side streets towards the highway. We can go down an exit ramp or climb down the embankment

22

maybe, but if I am remembering right it's mostly fence and steep as hell to get down to the pavement," I said. "You know before we get there you and I need to talk some more," I said while looking at him seriously.

"What, now David? I am starting to hate that look of yours. Every time you get it, I swear a black cloud starts rising up in back of you."

"Well, buddy, you're right. I got a lot more doom and gloom to share with you." I paused a moment to gather my thoughts. "Dump, we've been real lucky so far." I said and before I could carry on.

"Lucky? How? Getting a few cans of food and some water to wrap up in a smelly ass tarp?" he interrupted accusingly.

"No," I said in a calm soothing voice, "That not only was it lucky we were not in one of those car wrecks we have seen today, but we didn't have to decide whether or not to stop and help someone who was hurt in one." I let that sink in for a moment, before continuing. "Those cars on the interstate were traveling 55-70 mph when there engines shut off, there is going to be some horrible shit to see and possibly hear once we get down to it." I grimly told him.

"Man, we have died and gone to hell haven't we?" Dump hung his head and stated solemnly.

"We aren't dead yet and we got more options than a lot poor Son of Bitches do. I was just warning you that it is going to be rough, and that you might need to harden your heart a bit." I stood and said, "Come on, let's get started, it ain't getting any cooler standing baking in the sun here."

Dump started musing and said "David, do you know what a bitch is? I was going to take off today and get some work done in the garden."

"I sympathize with you," I told him, "I been planning for this the crap to hit the fan for years and all my prepper gear is scattered all over the place, just when I needed it most."

LAST SUPPER

"What's 'prepper gear'?" Dump inquired.

I`M A PREPPER YOURE A PREPPER TOO

Figure 12-9. Horseshoe pack.

"Well, you are a bit young to remember Y2K I guess. Back then, they used to call folks like me survivalists. There are a lot of people now a days Google searching for definitions of a 'Prepper'. The term "prepper" or "prepping" means a person or lifestyle that involves getting prepared for the worst while hoping for the best. A prepper is someone who is uncomfortable relying on others for the basics of survival and protection before and after a disaster.

"The terms like "preparations", "how to be prepared", or maybe "preparing for what's to come have a lot to do with the threats this troubled society faces. The majority of preppers are what folks would deem "normal" average people. They just plan ahead and prepare. That means you and I are Preppers and the emergency or disaster supplies we need are called "Preps". The types of preparations needed are Survival Kits, Food Storage, and Emergency Supplies to get you through a disaster.

"I had a bug out or get home bag stashed in my truck to help me through a disaster like this, but now I got to build me one as we go since I couldn't retrieve mine. I am now the ultimate displaced prepper." I tell Dump.

"Why are you calling yourself a displaced prepper?" He asks as my new devotee that's appreciative of my sharing of some survival wisdom.

"One form of displaced prepper," I explain, "is the one that evacuates an area and has his or her bug out gear with them, but the majority of their preps left behind, but that can take care of them selves for a while. The other is someone who has a prepper mentality and has just had all their preps lost or stolen and is as unfortunate in goods as those who have not prepared and are also struggling for survival with limited options in the same reality.

The Displaced Prepper however has something more tangible than those less fortunate that cannot be lost or stolen and that is knowledge. Preppers do not only devote themselves to buying emergency preparedness supplies and storing food, they also store knowledge and experience. I used to have a blog that examined the various ways that preppers can survive and thrive when they are displaced from their normal surroundings. I would talk and write about things like using a survival key ring for your EDC (every day carry) survival kit. I still had mine thank God in my pocket and fumbled it for additional reassurance before I went on with my discourse.

"Can I see it?" Dump said inquisitively.

"Sure, but later. Looks like we got trouble up ahead."

A couple of punk teenagers had a middle aged woman backing up fearfully and clutching a bottle of water up ahead. "If you won't give me that water I take it, Bitch!" one of them was threatening.

"HEY!" I yelled, "LEAVE HER THE HELL ALONE!"

They turned and saw me and Dump picking up the pace towards them and decided it wasn't healthy to stick around, so tried to saunter off. Dump yelled at them he was going to put a boot up their asses if they didn't get the hell out of here NOW! And the miscreants beat feet in the opposite direction.

A now deeply relived, but still anxious, woman leaned against the brick retaining wall in front of an old wood frame huge house. The rich folks and developers had been buying and fixing up these old formally edge of the city houses for years and they were now considered nouveau chic to a new generation of ladder climbing execs.

"Are you ok?" I asked noting she was visibly shaken and sweating profusely from the Georgia heat.

"Yeah, I just need to catch my breath for a second. Those delinquents scared the hell out of me. Thank you so much for chasing them off." she replied.

"My pleasure, Miss, damn fool kids need to show some respect." Dump said. I side glanced over at him and raised an eyebrow, mentally chastising him for taking all the credit in rescuing this damsel in distress.

She must have caught my glance at him, as she pointedly stated, "Well, I sure do thank both of you for coming along when you did. I was about to throw that bottle of water and try to run away, but in this heat I really wanted to hang on to it."

27

"I think they said it was going to get up to 96 degrees today." I offered.

"Where are you coming from?" Dump asked.

" I was on the interstate when everyone's cars just died all at once and I had me a hell of a white knuckle ride until my vehicle stopped moving." she said glancing about in the general direction we were headed.

"That's so weird, she said, what could have caused that to happen?" she queried. "Do you think it was aliens? "She said, looking at us skeptically.

Dump put on his best professor persona, well if you could call it that and said, "No ma'am. David here says he thinks that the sun had a CME or coronal mass injection, something about a Carrington event, its all very technical." he said with a seriously scholarly nod that looked like he got it from the scarecrow on the Wizard of Oz.

Her eyes got big, and she stuttered out, "Well, did the aliens cause that? I've seen on TV shows they could stop cars and electronics with some kind of weird beam. That's why those kids could get so close to me, I didn't see them coming, because I was looking up at the sky for a UFO or a mushroom cloud or something."

"No." I replied. "It's like a solar flare. Happened before in 1859 and fried all the telegraph lines then. NASA's been warning us for years that we were going to have a big event like this in 2012 or 2013, but these things are hard to pin point." I explained, while looking around to see what professor Dump Truck was up to. He had moved a few steps down the street and was watching the direction that our hoodlums had run off in.

"We best move on before they round up their Posse and come back." he said.

"Damn, I wouldn't put it past them, good thinking Dump." I said eyeing the area.

"What did you call him?" the woman asked, still thinking about aliens and eying my own personal mutant bodyguard.

"His street handle is Dump Truck, sort of a nickname, Call him Dumpie for short" I said as Truck ambled back over. That last name I had for my bar ape produced a beautiful smile and a giggled response.

"Well, hi and thanks, Dumpie." she cheerfully said and extended her hand to him.

I didn't think he could get anymore red faced than he was already but, she actually made him blush!

"Dump Truck is the bouncer or doorman for Pandora's Wreck. I guess you might say he takes the trash out, so the nickname fits." I said grinning.

"Oh, I get it. That's a cool name." She said.

"I am Melanie." she said and extended her hand to me.

"David. Hey, where are you headed?" I asked.

"Towards Cheshire Bridge." she said, looking hopeful at the thought of being escorted by two would be protectors.

"That's back about 5 miles from where we came from. It's not too bad that way at the moment." I told her not relishing the thought of even considering going back instead of onward to home.

"Uh… David." Dump started to remind me. I glanced around and had an idea.

"Yeah, we need to get off this street, come on with us, Melanie, if you want and we will move one street over back towards where you are heading and talk for a minute." I said.

I really needed to find out what was happening on the interstate and if we weren't there, when those heathens possibly came back, out of sight might be out of mind.

"I wouldn't mind an escort out of here, sounds like a plan to me." Melanie said.

"Let's do a little zig-zagging over to the next couple streets and confuse our trail a bit. I am not up for extra walking, but I like to be on the safe side."

"Good idea." they both almost simultaneously said.

"Dump, keep on looking around for some kind of weapon." I said.

"Been doing it, there ain't shit around when ya need it." he grumbled. That's true; we had been having our eyes peeled for anything from a stick to a brick all the way down the road so far. Time to take command here and get my charges thinking war zone and cautious movement through this jungle, a quick scan of the area offered lots of opportunities.

"Look, normally I would stay in the shadows and out of the middle of the street, but all these cars broke down in the middle of the road might have things we need." I said in my best pathfinder, military-like manner. I will the take point on the left side of the cars. Melanie, you go on the right side of them. And Dump, you watch our backs and look into storefronts occasionally." I said while looking for agreement to my newly found leadership role.

"What exactly are we looking for? I thought you wanted us to find something heavy or sharp as a possible weapon while we evaded those punks." Melanie asked.

"See if any of these cars have got keys in them. I want a tire iron or whatever else might be in the trunk." I replied.

"A tire iron sure would be nice." Dump said while looking devilishly in my direction. I shudder to think what an enraged Dump Truck with a lug nut loosener could do to a man's coconut and we all spread out to keep stepping and prowling for possibilities. I stopped for a minute to let everyone catch up with me.

"I do not like this folks; you notice how quiet this street is? I think most of these folks knew it was a bad area to begin with and just got the hell out of dodge, as soon as they broke down. It is a bit of a ghost town in this

30

older sector, but the run down appearance of this area tells me people are not likely to hang around on a good day." I murmured while looking down the street at the scattering of vehicles in various positions from parked to wrecked or just stalled out in the road.

"Ha! What's that my friends, I see something interesting come on." and stepped off towards my goal.

"A bug mobile?" You aren't going all Mc Gyver on us, Dave, are you?" Dump truck questioned, as I was opening the hatch on an Orkin Truck.

"I am not sure if they have what I want, but I think they got the equivalent of mace in here." I said while rummaging around in the back of the truck.

"Yup, just as I expected" I said producing a brand new can of Wasp spray.

"What do you do with that, light it?" Dump inquired getting interested in the can.

"Nope, this bottle of bug mace works on people, too. It's worse than pepper spray and has some components in it similar to nerve gas."

"I am glad you're on our side, Dave." Melanie said speculatively.

"Here, take this, its point and spray at the face, no instructions needed if we get cornered, but hide it in your purse as a surprise." I said, while handing her the can of industrial strength 'hoodlum' spray.

"It won't permanently blind them, will it?" Melanie asked, as she was gingerly handling the can.

"It's possible, but when push comes to shove; their intentions don't have a conscience, its best you lose yours, too." I said looking seriously at her.

"I guess the world really has gone to hell in a hand basket." she resolutely replied.

"Just consider them aliens and that can of Raid is something they are allergic to kind of like slugs and salt." I said with a grin.

"Good one, David." Dump said, as we shared grins all around.

"Come on. Folks, lets keep moving another block over, and we stay tight for now," I declared while still scanning cars, but focusing on just making it out of the area.

"I have wanted to get a tire iron all day, but most folks will take their keys with them to get back in the house when they abandon a vehicle." I said musing at loud.

"Where's your home, David?" Melanie asked.

"Montgomery, Alabama." I said dismally.

"Shit, you're a long ways from home. Where you headed now?" she replied looking horrified.

"Montgomery. Dumps getting off the hike in Newnan and I'm going to road march my ass there come hell or high water." I claimed.

"You must have been in the military. I haven't heard that term in years, except for my Daddy sharing war stories with his buddies." Melanie replied.

"Yeah, I was. Its funny how your vocabulary changes once you join up."

"Melanie, next block or two, it time for you to go right and us go left. I'm sorry, but we got to divide paths." I said trying to look consolingly at her. She stopped, dead in her tracks.

"What?" she blurted.

"I… I kind of thought you were helping Me." she tearfully addressed me.

"We are, but our paths follow different roads. I am sorry, darling, but we gotta go." I said sheepishly. I don't know her well enough to hug her or put an arm around her shoulder. I am always a disaster when it comes to women's emotions and my need to care and protect when it's not on familiar grounds, hell, even when it is.

"Ok, I understand." she said wiping tears away. "It's… it's…just all too much…and

I..." *Ah hell David just hug her, if she knocks the shit out of you for doing it just take it and apologize I thought and so I did. Damn, this woman is strong, I thought. That's why you don't get close to drowning people as I felt the death grip on me that was supposed to be a returned hug.* I am looking over her shoulder at Dump, who is looking at me as uncomfortable and confused as I am.

"I will be alright, thanks for what you have done." Melanie said, after releasing me and we all resumed the passage down the street.

"What kind of condition is the Interstate in, Melanie?" I asked.

"It's a mess, but not as many bad wrecks as you would think though. When the cars conked out most everyone just coasted to a halt. It was bizarre though, kind of like a slow motion carnival ride slowing down when the operator hits the switch" She said reflecting on the scene.

"Too bad we don't have an on switch; it's going to be getting pretty rough out here." Dump said in reply.

"Were going to be cutting over to interstate ramp in a bit Melanie, let me tell you a few things that might help you out in this situation."

"Hey, I need all the advice I can get; I would appreciate it." she said turning in my direction. I got to hand it to her, she had regained her composure a lot quicker than I thought possible.

"OK, first off, when you get home put a pot under every faucet you got and run the water. Your pipes should still have water in them. I don't know if they got around to shielding the emergency generators at the water company or not, but even if they did the generators will run out of fuel in a few days or weeks, max." I told her as she listened intently.

"Next, don't flush the toilet; you need the water in the back tank. Line the bowl with a garbage bag to do your business in or try finding a 5 gallon bucket with a lid"

"We back to out houses for awhile it looks like." Dump said.

"Yeah, sanitation is going to be really hard from now on." I replied.

A group of stragglers from the interstate started moving towards our direction. All were hot and disheveled-looking; a few were bleeding from cuts and bruises most likely from car wrecks.

"Be best to try traveling with one of these groups, Melanie, there's safety in numbers." I told her.

She nodded her agreement and said "You got time to give me some more tips before you go?"

"Sure, do you know about using bleach to purify water?" I inquired.

"I have heard of it, but I don't know how much to use." She said.

"Use 3 drops to a quart or a liter and 5 drops for a half gallon, as a general rule. You can add a couple drops more, if the water is really cloudy. Avoid using bleaches that contain perfumes, dyes and other additives."

"Ah hell, all I got is April fresh smelling Clorox." she cried.

"Don't use it in your drinking water, be ok to wash with. If you find some regular bleach, mix in thoroughly and allow it to stand for at least 30 minutes before using. (60 minutes if the water is cloudy or very cold)."

"If you got any Iodine tincture 5 drops per quart, when the water is clear will do the trick." I said.

"I got some of that" she smilingly said.

"Stuff doesn't taste good, but if you add any kind of vitamin C to it, it neutralizes the taste, but don't put it in until after the iodine has cleaned the water. Takes about 30 minutes to do that, the same as bleach" I explained.

"Ok, hold up a second I want to write that down, in case I forget." Melanie said, while fumbling in her purse. I noticed she eyed the can of Wasp spray.

34

but didn't comment further.

While she was taking notes, I watched the stream of weary travelers making their way up from the interstate. This is good for me, I guess, less folks on the road to contend with. They will probably be trickling in for days depending on where their cars broke down and the resolve of their owners to get home. I pondered how long it was going to take me to travel 180 miles by foot. Hell, I am going to beg borrow or steal me a bicycle first chance I get.

Dump brought me back to the moment by asking "You're not supposed to drink either one long term are you I heard, isn't that right, Dave?

"Yeah, that's right." I allowed, "Boiling is the best way or you can pasteurize it, too."

"How do you pasteurize it?" Melanie asked.

"Just leave that bottle you got in your purse, capped out in the sun for an hour or two depending on the weather. That will do it."

"I am going to run out of charcoal pretty quick as it is, that's a good tip, David." Melanie responded.

"Hydrogen peroxide will work too, but you use like 1/8th of a cup to a gallon." I advised.

"I have some of that too, but that sounds like a lot." Melanie said looking skeptical.

"Hey, that his job. He gets paid to know things like that." Dump said looking all indignant.

"Really, what do you do David?" asked Melanie.

Dump answered for me before I could object, "He is an emergency manager." he said beaming that his buddy was supposed to be a pro.

"Oh, that's wonderful, what's FEMA's plan to deal with this?" Melanie questioned.

Damn. Dump, I didn't want to have this conversation.

"Well, FEMA, I am sorry to say, really doesn't have a plan for something of this magnitude." I replied.

"That doesn't surprise me they didn't seem to have much of one for Katrina either." Dump said.

Melanie was looking all crestfallen and thoughtful.

"You mean FEMA won't be coming to help"?

"Not anytime soon. Oh, they will get around to organizing something eventually, a lot of military trucks might still work, but as far as I can tell without hearing any news, this disaster is mostly a worldwide event. Resources are simply overwhelmed."

I let that sink in for a bit and then continued. "You're pretty much left to your own devices for the next couple months." I said.

Dump looked like he might say, 'or forever' and I gave him a look that said to hush.

"The best things you can do right now are tribe up with friends or relatives and help each other get through this."

"I see.., any other tips?" Melanie asked.

"Well, water is your biggest short term problem at the moment; just remember your hot water tank has water in it that you can get out from its drain pipe." I could probably stand here all day feeding her various bits of survival knowledge, but that wasn't going to happen, I pondered what few other tidbits I could share before I moved on.

"People will start panicking in the weeks to come; you need to do something about your security." I said while looking at her questionably.

"Oh, I have a pistol at my house." Melanie responded.

"'Might be a good idea to start wearing it." I offered.

"Going to get that bad, Dave?" Melanie said glumly.

"Afraid so, there is always a criminal element in society that waits to take advantage of situations like this." I said ominously.

"Just stay alert for possible dangers, most people though actually come together for the common good after disasters though." I offered.

"You guys wanted to get

going, any other useful information before I tear up before our farewells." Melanie slowly said.

"Yes, you should pack a bag with stuff like you were going camping for a weekend and keep it handy. There are going to be a lot of open fires being used for cooking and candles for lighting now, so with no fire department to contend with any accidents or arson you might have to get away with just what you can carry if the neighborhood catches fire." I said.

We stared at each other for moment and Melanie said " I wish you well, Dave, and thanks for everything." she gave me a quick hug and turned to Truck and said, "Bye, Dumpie." and gave him a quick hug, too.

"Bye, Melanie, stay safe." Dump murmured.

"I will." she said turning towards a group of road weary travelers and stepped out of our lives.

MAD DOGS AND ENGLISH MEN
"Mad dogs and Englishmen Go out in the midday sun" Noel Coward Song

Dump and I started trudging down the on ramp to the interstate and noted that the people coming up from it had slowed to a trickle. It was deathly quite, nobody talked much, I guess the heat of the sun, the shock of it all, and just the drudge of having to keep on going no matter what took away all interest in conversation.

There were vehicles as far as the eye could see in every direction. The event happened somewhere around 12.30 in the afternoon. Dumps watch had stopped but for some reason the clip on style pocket watch I had was still working, maybe because it was because it was shock resistant and antimagnetic. My said it was 6.30, I am glad the sun chose summer to have its fit, because I would still have light until about 8 o'clock or so. If this shit had of happened in winter, I would be a whole lot more uncomfortable and at risk than I was now, so I guess I should count my blessings. Walking on pavement didn't make any cooler though even with the sun going down.

"Hey Dump. I am not as young as I used to be, we need to talk about where we are going to sleep tonight. I can't keep on at this pace." I said.

"Hey man I am getting beat too, what do you have in mind"? He replied.

"I figure we keep on for about an hour and then pick an underpass or crawl up under a truck or something. Hey, by the way this close to the city the pigeons sometimes build nests at underpasses." I offered.

"I figured we could just crawl in one these cars to take a snooze when we wanted." Dump said.

"We could, but most of these cars have electric windows so we would have too leave the doors open. It's going to be hotter than hell no matter what, so I suggest pulling the mattresses out of the sleeper cab of one of these 18 wheelers and just picking us a spot. I am not too worried about dogs yet, so we don't need to be that protected." I countered.

"That's a good idea, but what's this about dogs?" he asked.

A lot of people travel with their pets, so expect to see them on the road, but later on as this crisis escalates and when people can't feed them, thousands…maybe millions are going to get turned loose. Also, you see, when the riots and the death in the city is happening the dogs will learn to fed on the bodies, then in turn will acquire the taste for humans. Now you have a pack of wild dogs who consider you and your loved ones as food. They have no fear of man and will kill you to insure their own survival. Now, I'm not trying to scare you or cause unwarranted fears, but dogs are about to become a major problem in the upcoming months.

"I was talking to a buddy of mine named Buckshot about this problem once and his theory was that starving people will kill the dogs for food. I say sure, some will become food, but the average household that has guns has less then 50 rounds, although most survivalists or preppers will have much more. So, I think after the first week most people will be out of ammo. Then, the packs will rule. "I told Truck, just so he would get a feel for what's to come.

"Damn, David you are just full of good news today aren't you? But you're right; I can see it now as feral dogs are already a problem in Georgia. It's not uncommon to hear about packs of 25 or so." he said.

"I guarantee people will let their pets go to fend for themselves when the food runs out. Make sure you are ready to face this threat. What kind of Guns you got at home Dump?" I asked.

"I had a bit of trouble with the law and lost my rights to own any." he said disgustedly.

"Mind telling me what they got you for"? I said more for conversations sake than worry.

"No, well get ready to laugh, I stole a dump truck."

"Ha, you're shitting me! That's funny as hell, so *that's* where you got your handle?" I said chuckling.

"Yup, that's where I got my name from." he replied grinning.

"What's going on up ahead?' looking at bizarre sight for even a day like today off to the side of the road. A wiry little man was sitting in a lawn chair next to a road sign that had a piece of cardboard attached to it. I couldn't make out what the sign said yet though, and he had a camp fire going off to his right. As we got closer to him, I could make out the sign 'Water $1.00' *Do what?* I said to myself shaking my head.

"Good day, Gents, care for some tea?" the figure in the lawn chair called out in an evidently British accent. Dump and I looked at each other and wandered over to the apparition. Here was this guy in plaid shorts and a Hawaiian shirt with a floppy white hat, taking a kettle off his fire. "Teas, free; I have closed up shop for the day." He chirped.

"Are you really selling water for a $1.00?" Dump asked.

"Well, not really any more. Like I said, shop's closed. But, I was actually renting my cups, water's free." the man replied.

I looked off to his right and saw he had a wicker basket like people used to carry on picnics with 4 cups, some plates and what looked like the space for

40

the kettle he had next to his fire.

"Have a seat, if you have a mind to, and I will tell you all about it. "He said, gesturing towards a bit of embankment.

"I got to hear this story and tea would be welcome." I said plopping down after un-slinging my pack. Dump did the same and we stared intently at the odd looking character waiting for him to begin.

"You see, I was coming back from vacation in Florida when this mess began, and like everyone else had to start walking home. Well, I grabbed my kit and got this far, when I spied that Collagen truck over there that contains 5 gallon bottles of water. Well, I think to me self, I don't really have a home here in Atlanta and I will need me a bit more money. So, I hit on a plan to help my fellow travelers and make a bit of scratch on the side." he said offering two cups of steaming tea to me and Dump on this hot summers day in the middle of nowhere.

"What I been doing is not stealing water mind you, I been renting my cups for $1.00 and all the water a body could drink." he said with a wise smile and a nod in his audiences direction.

"Hey, I got overhead, I washed those cups between clients." he replied, as Dump was looking at his cup like it had something wrong with it.

"So, I been picking me up a few quid to help on expenses once I get to Atlanta." the little man said proudly.

"If you want creamer or sugar I got some here, that water truck must have been stocking office buildings." he offered.

"Well, aren't you the resourceful one." I said admiring his ingenuity.

"You look pretty resourceful yourself, those are painters tarps aren't they?" he replied studying our improvised carry alls.

"Yeah, we are making do until we get home; although it looks to me that the road is our home for the next few days." I said with a sigh. "I got a lot further to go, but maybe I will get off the road here and there." I continued thoughtfully.

"You said you didn't really

have a home in Atlanta, what did you mean?" Dump asked the Brit.

"I live in London; I only come over for a bit of holiday. I am hoping the Embassy will take me in, when I get into the city." he said more cheerily than I think he meant.

"Wow, Dave, I thought you had it bad." Dump said while looking at our strange host.

"He got stuck in a whole another country, because of this EMP crap." Dump said decidedly.

"EMP!? Yes, that's what I thought it might be. Any news if it be natural or nuclear? "The Englishman said.

"I am guessing natural based on the last time I saw a space weather report. But, who knows?" I replied.

"You know about EMP?" Dump directing his attention to our traveler.

"I know a bit, not much mind you, but I have done some reading, my name is Stewart by the by. " Said the Brit.

"Mine's David and this here is Dump Truck." I said pointing in Dumpie's direction.

"Glad to meet ya both. Is that Dump Truck, as in the vehicle?" Stewart asked suppressing a chuckle.

"It's Dump Truck, as in Bar Bouncer." I replied.

"Oh, good show! That is amusing!" proclaimed Stewart eyeing my rotund companion.

I was dying to tell the real reason he got that name, but decided to have mercy on Dump.

"So, I see you been here a bit to make a camp." I said looking about. He had pieces of old pallet, various sticks and bits of lumber piled up for fire building. Had what looked to be a spread rolled up for his bedroll?

"If you want a chair, there is a pickup truck about 50 yards down the road that has some lawn chairs in the back." Stewart offered.

"Maybe later, I need some shade right now; I am thinking,

and as far away from this fire as I can possibly sit." I said looking around.

"There is a flat bed over there with a tarp over some equipment. Let's make an awning Dump." I declared and headed on over with Dump in tow.

We got the tarp off and rigged it to the side of the van containing Stewart's stash of water jugs and sundries.

"You boys made me a right proper kiosk, you did!" Stewart announced admiringly.

"I made me some shade, I don't know how you can sit out in the sun so close to that fire." I replied laughing.

"Kind of dumb isn't it? To be honest with you, I was counting my money when you blokes came walking up and didn't have time to hide it other than sitting upon it." he said sheepishly, then standing up to reveal a small pile of cash and coin.

Dump started chuckling as Stewart grabbed up a couple fists full of dollars and said, "Business must have been good!"

"Aye Mate. that it was." Stewart admitted laughingly in response.

"I was getting hot as hell over there, but times being what they are you can't be too careful." he jovially said and I guess just trusting us over remaining by that fire for one more minute.

"You had any problems with your clients today, Stewart?" I chimed in.

"Oh, a few bloody assholes, but most folks thought my cup rental notion was funny and paid me right and proper, rather than trying to drink out of a 5 gallon bottle. Like I said, the water is free." he smirked.

"It's going to be getting dark soon and I kind of like your little camp here. Would you mind if we stay overnight' I asked.

"Make yourselves to home, gents. And, I would be appreciating the company of such handy and hardy chums." Stewart replied dragging his chair back under the shade.

" I guess, seeing that we are
43

teaming up for the night, Dump and I are going to throw our packs under this van while we do a bit of foraging, and you can sort of watch out for them while you wait on a customer to come along." I said while Dump looked at him suspiciously.

"Like I said, store's closed for now, I want to look around a bit, too; but I think they will be alright either way." Stewart said standing up.

"Oh, I am funny about leaving my preps unguarded; I will just drag them along. Where did you say that lawn furniture was at Stewart?" I said while picking up my roll.

"It is that blue truck down there about 50 meters that way." he said gesturing toward a pickup.

"Ok, anything else of the interesting sort down that way?" I inquired.

"I didn't look over everything properly and only stayed on this side of the median." Stewart replied scanning the area.

"Well, I see a couple big rigs down there. I was telling Dump that we could drag the mattresses out of the sleepers and rest a little easier tonight." I said motioning in their general direction.

"Capitol idea! I hadn't thought of that one." Stewart said.

"Well, we will meet you back at camp in a bit or see you around the area. I am going after some chairs first. Come on along Dump." I said while slinging my pack once again over my aching shoulder.

"Hey, Stewart, while you're up in the cab of one of those trucks, be looking for a tire thumper." I informed him.

"What in the hell is a tire thumper?" Stewart asked regarding me quizzically

"It's a 'billy-club' or a bat that truckers use to check inflation of their tires, they use it to beat on them." I offered.

"I'll be damned, I never heard of one, but a proper nightstick sounds like just the thing I might be wanting." Stewart replied, and we all looked at each other suspiciously about spending the night with an armed stranger.

I diffused the moment by

adding, "'Might be useful if you get anymore asshole customers." and laughed.

"Yes, a Tommy knocker would be just the thing for adjusting bad attitudes." Stewart replied with a grin relaxing a bit.

Dump and I started heading off towards the pickup with the chairs and I kept noticing the discarded brief cases, clothes and luggage dumped on the sides of the road by travelers unwilling to further carry their burdens.

"Hey Dump, you notice how much more women's junk is strewn around than men's stuff?' I observed while surveying a dizzying array of bright colors and various high heeled shoes littering the highway.

"I noticed that, too. 'Looks like women packed too much and it only took a mile or so until they started dumping shit." he replied.

"I hope most of them carried an extra pair of sensible shoes in their cars like Melanie did or they are going to be hurtin' for certain." I considered.

"I wonder how she is making out; I was getting to like that old girl." Dump responded.

"Old! Hell Dump, she was younger than me. Ha! I sort of thought you were attracted to her." I jibed at him.

"I didn't say she wasn't attractive." he stammered.

'Makes you sort of wish we got her phone number or something if this shit ever gets back on track doesn't it Dumpie'

Dump looked remorseful and murmured, "You think it ever will David?"

"Doubtful Dump, I just don't know. It is a different world now, but civilization always comes back and forms some kind of balance after a disaster. Though there's no telling' how long it'll take."

"Well, I hope she is alright." Dump considered.

"I do too, my friend." I replied.

AND IT'S PARTY TIME

Dump and I hauled back some folding chairs to camp and looked around for Stewart. He waved at us from the other side of the median while dragging a mattress back and stopped and reached in his belt and held up a Billy club. Dump gave him thumbs up and we turned to resume our foraging.

"I claim that Peterbilt up ahead." I informed Dump.

"Damn! I was going to put dibs on that, but you beat me to it. Probably got better shit in it than those cheaper trucks." He groused.

"Ah Dumpie that looks like a Mack or a Kenworth in the other lane, pickings should be just as good over there' I responded.

"I was just kidding, I will see you in a few." he said walking over to the other side of the eight lane highway we were traversing, eight, hell it was 16 lanes, eight on a side. Damn Atlanta has some major thorough fares and this bit we were on had lanes full of vehicles of every description.

I approached the truck and reminded myself just as a precautionary measure to beat on the side of the door, in case it was occupied. Might sound dumb in this turmoil; but I didn't need to be looking at the wrong end of a 44 magnum, if this guy decided he wanted to stay with his load for some reason. *I should have told Dump and Stewart to take the same precaution I pondered.*

No answer to my knock and the driver left it unlocked, cool. I opened the door and climbed in. I hadn't considered until now that it's second nature for a lot of drivers to lock their cars, when they got out up until now and considered myself lucky I didn't have to try every truck on the interstate to put my bed idea to good use.

Damn, this truck is ritzy; he has got him a TV, microwave, refrigerator and all the comforts of home in this thing, including a computer. Tire thumper, tire thumper, where's the friggin tire thumper. Must of took it with him, that's a no brainier I would have too, unless I had a gun with me. L.O.L., knowing me, I would have carried 'em both.

What kind of shit you got in that chest of drawers? I mused reaching to open .a drawer Sweet! A whole new pack of white socks, damn do I need those. What else we got, manicure kit with comb, ok that's got my name on it, double AA batteries, yea I want those, Viagra well that's barter material, caffeine tablets might need those, who the hell writes their name on their underwear and size 42 at that, don't need those, maybe Dumpie might want them,,,, hee hee. Instant coffee packets! Hell yea! Damn, empty snack drawer.

Let me unbutton this mattress from the cabs bed, well you left me the sheets and I damn sure don't need a blanket at the moment. I prefer my tarp thank you if I get stuck I the rain. "What's this" I say as I spy an envelope, Yee hah! $500 in fifties, guess you had other things on your mind to forget this, but your loss is my gain as I grinned and begin to back out of the cab of the truck dragging the mattress and the rest of my loot in a pillow case. I was reaching back in the cab for the pillow that went with it when I faintly heard Dump hollering at me.

"David! David!" he was bellowing like an excited water

buffalo. I walked around to the front of the truck and saw Dump gesturing at me from across the median.

"Come here, you ain't going to believe this!" he was shouting with some enthusiasm.

"Ok, on my way" I yelled back and proceeded in his direction.

"What's up" I inquired while approaching him.

"Take a gander at this" he said all beside himself with glee.

"What is it?" I kept repeating as I jumped the median barrier and hurried towards him.

"Come around here!" he cried, while moving around the front of the big rig that he had just dragged a mattress and some other goods out of.

"Ok! Ok! I am coming!" I yelled back as I rounded the front of the truck to see Dump standing there grinning and doing a magicians 'wah la' motion towards a….

"Beer truck!" I hollered in response.

"Beer truck" Dump reaffirmed proudly, puffing out his chest.

"And you don't have the doors open already, where's your manners?" I joked hurrying towards it.

"Damn thing is locked." he said to my dismay.

"Shit. Tire tool maybe?" I said raising an eyebrow.

"We haven't had much luck acquiring one of those." he stated.

"Hang on" I said eying the lock down chains on the back of the rig he had got his mattress from.

"We might can knock the padlock off with one of those or make it spring." I said hopefully.

"I got just the ticket possibly." Dump said and went back around the front of the truck and produced somebody's country craftsmanship of a trailer hitch topping off about two foot of what appeared to be a hickory mattock handle.

"Damn that's a nasty looking weapon, look here lemme see that." I said reaching for the deadly looking tire thumper.

"Watch this shit and learn a new trick, Dumpie" I confirmed my intent to get into the beer truck by whacking the outside edge of the padlock.

"Man you can't beat that thing off. "Dump said skeptically.

"Hell I can't" I responded and gave it another whack.

"You see, Dump. I got practice at this. When someone loses a key to their locker in the Army, you got two choices to get in it. A Drill Sergeant's key which is a well worn pair of bolt cutters or, as I have done, hit it with the back of an axe. If you hit it just right next to the top of where the locking mechanism of the bar is, it will spring open." I explained, while renewing my efforts and causing a spark to fly.

"This damn thing is rounded so I can't get a good lick on it, give me a second." I said while beating on the lock unmercifully.

"Ka Ching!' the lock busted.

"In like Flynn." I boasted raising the door to the bin holding my goodnight medicine.

"Well, I'll be damned!" Dump said, reaching for a hot one.

I grabbed one and we both popped the tops and made various exclamations about not liking hot beer, but it sure tasted good at the moment, while we were leaning against the side of the truck.

"Hey, we found Stewart a new business." I said laughing.

"Yeah, Man! He can open a new bar out here; call it the Red Neck Riviera!" Dump exclaimed.

"Ha, and you could bounce and I could collect the money." I chuckled.

"Seriously, though Bro, we got to watch the beer tonight, because we're going to be sweating bullets and dehydrating come tomorrows walk." I said.

"No problem, I am aware of that." Dump said while trying to get a glimpse over the divider to the next bin.

"Hey, there are bottles over there. You reckon Stewart has a bottle opener?" he guffawed.

"If not I might sell him one." I chuckled.

"Minus the service fees for opening the door for him, of course." Dump said grinning.

"Hey, there should be a hand truck shoved under the back of this thing lets go get it." I replied.

"Damn, Davie boy you don't miss a trick do you." Dump responded while walking towards the back of the vehicle with myself tagging along.

"Try not to, but I can't think of any 'hand truck' jokes at the moment." I said trying to get a rise out of him about his nickname.

"You're a smart ass Dave, a funny smart ass, but a smart ass all the same." he told me while dragging the hand truck out from under the bumper at the back of the truck.

"How much beer you want to grab?" he said while pulling a case off the stack.

"Grab one more and that ought to do us, but I am going to reach over in that other bin just to get a bottle and share some jokes with Stewart." I quipped while crawling into the cavernous, but oven like interior of the truck.

We loaded up our mattresses, beer and whatever else goods would fit on the hand truck and proceeded back towards Stewart's Camp with me carrying my pillow case and Dumpie playing my pack mule.

"Yo, Stewart, the guests have arrived." I hollered up to the sight of Stewart adding some more debris to his fire. *What's up with him keeping that damn thing going as hot as it is I wondered?*

""You look like you did well!" he hollered back at the sight of me toting a bag and Dump following my charge with an over loaded hand cart.

"That we did!" I responded. "Might even have a surprise for you, too!" I suggested teasingly.

"Well, I got one for you, too!" He hollered back.

We rolled into camp and noticed Stewart had carefully lined up a few bottles of coke and

50

some boxes of peanut butter crackers and other savory bits from a vendors truck in front of our fold up chairs.

"Well, are you not the best host in the world!" I exclaimed at his efforts.

"That's nice." Dump said as he parked the haul to the side.

"Is that beer I spy?" Stewart said, as he shuffled towards Dump trucks unloading efforts.

"Sounds good don't it," as Dump proceeded to hand him a case.

As Stewart was setting the case of beer cans down and smiles were flashing all the way around, I produced a bottle of beer out of my back pocket and held it up for his inspection.

"I got one." He said producing a church key and having a belly laugh.

"Spoil sport." I opined, "I have been regaling Dump with all the good jokes we could have at your expense, if you didn't." I said lustily smirking and cracking open my own brew with my own bottle opener.

"Now, if you have a can opener about your person, *then* we could talk." Stewart countered.

"Oh, I got one all right." I said producing my infamous key ring, as well as digging in my pocket for my knife. "But these are not for sale." I told him explicitly.

"Kind of like me with my cups, if you missing one element it's hard to partake." Stewart shot back.

"Two is one and one is none. As we used to say in the military." I interjected.

"Good saying. Makes one think about what happens if you lose something." Dump said going into his Professor Gogglestein interpretation.

"It's weird what we come to value or help us survive at this moment, is it not Dave?" said Stewart deliberating.

"I can tell you a trick to an opening a can when you lack a can opener, though that might be useful if you find yourself in that situation." I offered.

"Please, do tell." Stewart said with some interest.

"There is a survivalist named Cody Lundin that taught me this trick, you can scrape or wear the edge off a can by sort of polishing it on the curb of the street, if you absolutely had to." I explained and told him in further depth the technique to separate the solder joint of a can.

"Why do you keep messing with that fire Stewart? It's not buggy yet." Dump said as the Englishman added, yet again, more fuel to the fire, that just seemed to further our discomfort.

"It will be dark soon and I do not have matches to spare to light another." Stewart said contemplating.

"I bet Dave has got a fire trick or two to consider when you run out of matches." with a nod to my direction. And they both turned towards me still sipping their suds.

"Well, you ought to be able to scavenge some matches if you look in likely places; but ok , I got a trick or two to share other than the obvious ways to make fire the normal way using lighters and such or being reduced to friction." And I explained:

Balloons and Condoms

By filling a balloon or condom with water, you can transform these ordinary objects into fire creating lenses.

Fill the condom or balloon with water and tie off the end. You'll want to make it as spherical as possible. Don't make the inflated balloon or condom too big or it will distort the sunlight's focal point. Squeeze the balloon to find a shape that gives you a sharp circle of light. Try squeezing the condom in the middle to form two smaller lenses.

Condoms and balloons both have a shorter focal length than an ordinary lens. Hold them 1   to 2 inches from your tinder.

AND IT'S PARTY TIME

Fire from Ice

Fire from ice isn't just some dumb cliché used for high school prom themes. You can actually make fire from a piece of ice. All you need to do is form the ice into a lens shape and then use it as you would when starting a fire with any other lens. This method can be particularly handy for wintertime camping.

Get clear water. For this to work, the ice must be clear. If it's cloudy or has other impurities, it's not going to work. The best way to get a clear ice block is to fill up a bowl, cup, or a container made out of foil with clear lake or pond water or melted snow. Let it freeze until it forms ice. Your block should be about 2 inches thick for this to work.

Form your lens. Use your knife to shape the ice into a lens. Remember a lens shape is thicker in the middle and narrower near the edges.

Polish your lens. After you get the rough shape of a lens, finish the shaping of it by polishing it with your hands. The heat from your hands will melt the ice enough so you get a nice smooth surface.

Start a fire. Angle your ice lens towards the sun just as you would any other lens. Focus the light on your tinder nest and watch as you make a once stupid cliché come to life.

The Coke Can and Chocolate Bar

I once saw this method in a YouTube video some time ago and thought it was a pretty slick trick. All you need is a soda can, a bar of chocolate, and a sunny day.

Polish the bottom of the soda can with the chocolate.
Unwrap your bar of chocolate and start rubbing it on the bottom
of the soda can. The chocolate acts as a polish and will make the
bottom of the can shine like a mirror. If you don't have
chocolate with you, toothpaste also works.

Make your fire. After polishing the bottom of your can, what
you have is essentially a parabolic mirror. Sunlight will reflect
off the bottom of the can, forming a single focal point. It's kind
of like how a mirror telescope works.

Point the bottom of the can towards the sun. You'll have
created a highly focused ray of light aimed directly at your
tinder. Place the tinder about an inch from the reflecting light's
focal point. In a few seconds you should have a flame.

While I can't think of any time that I would be in the middle
of nowhere with a can of Coke and chocolate bar, this method is
still pretty cool.

Batteries and Steel Wool

Like the chocolate and soda can method, it's hard to imagine
a situation where you won't have matches, but you will have
some batteries and some steel wool. But hey, you never know.
And it's quite easy and fun to try at home.

Stretch out the Steel Wool. You want it to be about 6 inches
long and a ½ inch wide.

Rub the battery on the steel wool. Hold the steel wool in
one hand and the battery in the other. Any battery will do, but 9

volt batteries work best. Rub the side of the battery with the "contacts" on the wool. The wool will begin to glow and burn. Gently blow on it.

Transfer the burning wool to your tinder nest. The wool's flame will extinguish quickly, so don't waste any time.

"You want simpler" I said sensing I was losing my audience in contemplation. "Make a small hole in any paper sheet, spit in this hole or put a clear water drop that you present to the sun rays as a magnifying glass."

"That's brilliant Dave, you're a regular pyromaniac. You can make fire out of a drop of water and that coke can shit is unbelievable." Stewart said.

Dump was beaming,"I told you he knows some weird stuff that's useful; you just got to put up with him long enough to listen." he said playfully towards me.

"I am going to hush for awhile. Dump you feel like playing bartender and giving us another round?" I said hopefully.

"Not a problem my, friend." he said and reached down beside him to contribute to our getting inebriated.

"Hey, this hot beer doesn't taste so bad." said Stewart.

"Coming from an Englishman that somehow sounds funny." I wise cracked.

"We drink it hot, we drink it cold, we like our pints and not necessarily warm, that's a myth." he responded.

"You are opening the store tomorrow?" Dump asked Stewart with a sly grin and a reach for another beer.

"Hell, why not when I got so much free stock to profit from." Stewart replied with mirth.

"I gotta go use your facilities Stewart, where is the John at" I asked nonchalantly,

"Over there, pick a patch of weeds" Dump suggested.

"Anybody find any toilet

paper today?" I speculatively asked.

"I got some." Stewart said rummaging in his own pillow case and handing me a roll, "Dump when you get to Dave and my` age remember the old adage 'never trust a fart'."

Dump responded right on time with "I trust you" and I stayed amused by this statement, as I headed to my destination on the far side of the road.

.

Fare Thee Well

"Dave, I been telling Stewart about looking out for dogs in the future" Dump said as I wandered back into camp and their gaze shifted in my direction.

"Two legged and four legged types will all be packing up soon" I said wearily.

"I am not sure which kind will first but form packs they will. Those are not firecrackers we been hearing off and on all day' I said gesturing towards the gloom and twinkling fires off in the city.

"I thought you said regardless what the media said about people during Katrina that your college research said it was just hype and outright lies" Dump said looking intently at me.

"Your correct Dump, but that was a different disaster. Oh, most folks will get along for a couple weeks until the water and food run out, and then it starts getting every man for himself. Now, in the interim, a lot of the more, shall we say 'criminal elements' will try to take advantage of the situation to get what they want, be it by looting or an opportunity for revenge on whoever they think has wronged them." I said grimly.

"I guess the street gangs are going to have a field day; if they don't kill each other off." Dump offered.

"Well, they will be settling their differences as usual, but the problem with them is they already have leadership and a pack they belong to already. We can hope they kill each other off some, but they will start organizing and expanding turf long before that, I am afraid. You see we are now in what is called a WROL situation, that means "without rule of law" I explained.

"You Yanks I always heard were armed to the teeth; sounds like its going to be a bloody war zone." Stewart said disgustedly.

"It beats the blood bath that's going to happen in your country, Stewart. Your government disarmed the populace. How are the regular folks going to defend themselves?" Dave aimed in his direction.

"Yeah, seems I heard London is about half Muslim or foreigners now, and on top of that you got your own gang problems." Dump said pointedly.

"Then, you got your soccer thugs that like to fight and play anarchist." I offered.

"Too right! Too Bloody well, right! There's going to be mayhem aplenty alright. In me own homeland, the Bobbies can't take care of gangs now, let alone the 'mayhem' this whatever it is that has come upon us." Stewart said angrily.

"Gangs run like military organizations and since enlistment ranks were low, we have let too many gang bangers into the military by lowering standards and they have brought back what they learned from that training to the streets." I said ominously while reaching for another hot beer.

"Hey, guys, I don't have the energy for it, but if someone wants to get a Co2 fire extinguisher off one of the vehicles around here we can have cold beer" I said hopefully.

"I ain't getting up, but I want to know how it's done" Dump said with an eye towards Stewarts direction.

"Me neither, I am worn out, but do go on with the story David" Stewart said almost apologetically.

"Well when I was in the Field Artillery we used to take one

58

of those red carbon dioxide fire extinguishers off one of the tracked cannons and put the beer in a duffel bag and, WHOOSH! Cold beer I said laughing.

"Cool, would a pillow case work" Dump said contemplating.

"Should, but those duffels were sort of nylon canvas material, I don't know if it would work or not, because cotton is pretty porous" I said trying to envision what might happen or not happen.

"Well, I'm not volunteering now, at the moment mind you, but I would be willing to give her a try later." Stewart said rubbing the stubble where his beard was soon to be.

"I am just glad enough to be quit moving at the moment." I declared and got assenting comments all around.

"Guys, I am not too worried about anyone invading our camp tonight, because this disaster is young; but let's talk a bit about that, because I want to go to sleep soon." I said speculatively to my bunk mates.

"I been thinking about that, I will take a watch if you want David." he offered in my direction and glanced over at an attentive Stewart.

"Well, I don't see a high risk of an unguarded camp, but let's kick it a bit. I think we need as much rest as we can get, while we can, and others coming our way if we let this fire go out won't even know we are here, if they pass in the night." I said considering the possibilities.

"Light discipline is a must, no telling what kind of moths will come to our flame if we were all sleeping. "Dump said looking pointedly towards Stewart's passion for building bonfires.

"Dumpie, how long you been listening to Blake and crew kicking it?" I chortled.

"Light suppression," I said laughing out loud "is one of those terms we bandy about, when I am not supposed to be smoking a cigarette at night." I stated while firing me up.

Dump got a devilish grin on his face, made worse due to the flickering flames of the campfire in back of him and responded with, "They say a sniper can see you light cig at a mile at night." Dump produced from his overheard stash of soldier lore.

'That's a fact Truck; I used to have to hide under a poncho to keep smoking these damn things before. Hey! Has anyone seen a cigarette truck, out here anywhere?" I said producing a loud laugh out of Stewart. He held up a crumpled half pack of smokes

"I was on the look out for one and had half of mind to try to charge you for these, but seeing that we are all brethren of the coast now, like a bunch of pirates, you may have them free with my compliments." he said passing them over to me.

"Thank you, Stewart!" I exclaimed not even bothering to make remark about the brand name and deposited them in my shirt pocket.

"That just earned you a new pair of socks. I was going to wrestle a dollar out of you for... Rental, mind you; like leasing shoes at the bowling alley." I said smiling.

"Damn! Show you two a street corner and I bet you would own it in a week." said Dump grinning.

"Stewart, you don't really have anywhere to go, you want to consider joining the Dump Truck Tribe? I need a resourceful soul like you. My last statement took Dumpie unawares and he turned to Stewart and said, "Come on the more the merrier! The Truck Tribe, I like that, awful nice of you David." he said beaming in my direction.

"How about it, Stewart?" I asked.

An uncomfortable Stewart squirmed in his chair and responded after a momentary pause.

"Gents, I am honored to be asked, and kindly fellows you are to have a use for an old man, but my travels need to be towards my kith and kin, if I ever want to see the shores of my own land again." he carefully said with what looked like to be a tear welling up in his eye in this dim light.

"Stewart, do you have much family back home?" I softly asked, recognizing he was

60

troubled.

"Well, me Mum and Da both passed awhile back, but I have my connections and my heart back home; as I guess we all have our obligations and friends needing us about now." he replied suppressing a show of emotion among men towards tears.

"Yes, my friend, I got worries and responsibilities a plenty too, that I sort of put out of my mind till now." I said dolefully.

"Let's talk about some brighter things and consider our dinner for the night, what's everybody willing to share for the pot?" I inquired digging in my improvised pillow case bag for some Campbell's chicken noodle soup.

"Hey, I got two of those." said Dump producing his scavenging out of a similar sack, all the while looking like a bald, beardless, tattooed Santa Claus.

"I got ZILCH in the soup department, but I foraged us up a good fry pan out of a car over there, that has some more pots and pans in it." Stewart said producing it.

"Well, it might taste a bit nasty, but for foods sake, Dump and I got a couple of cans of Tuna to add to it, so we got something to stick to our ribs past noon tomorrow." I suggested.

"I just as soon have the soup and Beer." Dump countered making a face.

"I am in agreement." Stewart said looking similar to Dumps grimace of my culinary suggestion.

"Fine by me, but your belly is going to be touching your backbone soon enough and it won't sound so bad." I made them recognize, but did get in agreement that it was a bad idea for this evening.

"David, you want to stay with me awhile when we get to Newnan? Now, before you object, I got plenty of relatives living mostly close and they would take you in on my say so and you could restock and regroup a bit." he said inquiringly.

"That's awful nice of you Dump, and I may yet take you up on that, but I gotta get home. Can we talk more on the prospect" I said while not burning any bridges.

"Sure, just want you to consider it" he said forgiving an outright refusal of hospitality and possible stupidity on my part.

"We got a long road up ahead, Dump, all options are on the table, and I am thankful for your generosity, but I got folks needing me that are on my mind." I said wistfully.

"Understood." is all he said.

We all contemplated the fire light in silence for a bit, and the possible or improbable need to smother this soothing fire at the moment.

"Dump, can we go country route from here and get off the main drag?" I said, considering what I needed to explain next.

"Oh yeah, I been thinking about that, we can get off at the, uh, I think next or the one after that exit to head in my direction, but it's out of the way for you." he said studying me.

"I have some worries what an exit is going to look like off this maze." I declared, thinking about my next statement before I carried on. "It's going to look like a rock concert or a flash mob as folks wander in, and overwhelm what ever resources might be there" I suggested.

Stewart considered this possibility and its ramifications for a moment. "David, what do you think the world trade center downtown Atlanta is going to look like come next week"? He said cautiously.

"Going to be hell, Stewart, every foreigner from every country is going to try to make their way there that got stranded in the city or highway." I let that sink in for a moment.

"Stewart, not to alarm you, but make you aware; people that are different from mainstream in society start to get hated for whatever reason, after a disaster if recovery is not quick." I said sympathetically, but directly.

"Shit, I am no better than a Paki blighter in this town, then." Stewart said, thinking about his colonial roots and problems caused in his own cites. He went on further, looking off in the distance, as he could envision Koreans, Chinese, Spanish, Japanese, Pakistanis, etc. all converging on one spot in a myriad of languages and confusion and being set upon by the locals, like this was somehow their fault or that they were not worthy of the same respect as humans as those that had more historic roots in the area.

"Dump, could you, I mean, would you give me your address in case I need to, what did you call it Dave, "Bug out" if it gets too bad?" Stewart said pleadingly.

"No problem, welcome to the Dumpie clan, if you need too, oops Tribe, right David?" He said extending his oversize mitt in Stewart's direction, which was received and shook heartily.

"Let me find a bit of paper and pencil.' Stewart said, while rummaging in his luggage.

"David, I got an old spinster cousin on the outskirts of Newnan. We should be able to make it to in a day or so, if we going the back way. "Dump said speculatively.

"A rest and a friendly face a day or two from now, might just be exactly what we need to recharge our batteries, my friend." I said in agreement.

"Stewart, I'll draw you map, or better yet, we find a regular road map in the morning and I will mark a route out." Dump said turning towards the older Brit and grabbing another can of suds.

Almost simultaneously, Stewart and I said we had maps from today's treasure hunt.

"You know that's kind of dumb of me not to pick one up, just because I knew where I was headed." Dump said a bit apologetically.

"Gotta think ahead. Right, Dave? Home may be where the map tells you, not your senses, I think you said." He said eying the cans of soup sitting on the ground in front of him.

"Always have an alternate route and be ready with a detour at the worst possible moment is a plan indeed Dumpy." I replied

63

while digging out my key ring.

"You know how to use a P38 Truck"? I inquired producing one and handing it over for his inspection.

"Heard of them but never played with one" he replied unfolding the tiny can opener attached to the key chain.

" Give her here , I know about such" said Stewart and half opened a can as a demonstration before passing it back to Dump to finish and practice on,

"Hell that's about as quick as a regular one" Dump said gleefully reaching for another to start on.

"Its all in the wrist, once you master the technique there is nothing to it." Stewart said reaching for the opened can and pouring the contents into his fry pan.

"Tell me a bit about your cousin Dump"/ I inquired.

"Well she is big as a house but not hard to look at" he began before Stewart and I started laughing at his description.

"Runs in the family" I said smirking at Dump

"See I told you he was a smartass" Dump said to Stewart handing him the other can but not taking any offense.

" She's had many a suitor but lives at the old family place by herself and just well, likes it that way and aged enough that men don't come around much anymore" He said describing his relative.

"Hell of a cook though, Dave, if there's something left to cook after the refrigerator and freezer turned off Dave, you're in for a feast. She's raising chickens though so I reckon we eat either way" he declared.

"Sounds like a winner to me! How far do you think her place is"? I questioned trying to discern the map in the dim light.

"I dunno... 8 or 12 miles. It's a bitch to think about hoofing it versus driving it." He contemplated.

"Well one day's forced march" I offered.

"Probably, but you said something about staying out of the noon day sun and walking more at dusk like we were in the desert ' He countered.

"Well if we got a destination in mind we don't have to pace ourselves that strictly "I contemplated.

"We will be there by 7 or 8 at night if we just take it light" I said hopefully.

"I am figuring about the same" Dump said rubbing his feet.

"Soups on" said Stewart digging in his picnic basket for some bowls and pouring straight out of the pan a portion for each of us.

"Don't need to soil a spoon I will just sip it out of the bowl with my beer" Dump said.

"Even though at the moment we got lots of water to wash with, I second that" I declared.

"We going to leave at first light or as soon as I wake up Stewart. As us country boys say, I feel like I been road hard and put up wet" I said venting how tired I was but I don't think Stewart understood my saying. The party continued on for awhile and despite my own admonishment not to over indulge we did and I woke to the sun rising with the mung head.

"Wake up call Dump, I said to my traveling partner who appeared to my bleary eyes to be a beached whale.

Stewart stirred and sat up remarking "Blimey the world ends and we still gotta go to work"

"Dump. Wake your big ass up buddy." I said nudging him.

"I am awake, I just can't move yet "Dump said rising up on one elbow blinking at the sun.

"Its early as hell and getting hot already" he moaned.

"Anybody wants some coffee" I offered

"You will not be putting that foul brew in me pot" said Stewart reaching for his tea pot.

"Hey compromise buddy, I just need some hot water and I am in charge of remaking the fire" I said staggering to my feet,

"That's right you got instant, sorry it's just that I got my pot seasoned just right" Stewart said while regaining his own feet.

"Dump you think that cousin of yours is going to object to some night visitors" I said

"Do what"? He replied still trying to orient himself.

"She ain't going to take a pot shot at us appearing after dark in the middle of this shit is she" I explained.

"Oh, no, she probably just thinks the powers out and hasn't even tried her car yet, she don't get out much." He said moving the Van as he used it for support to get up.

"Damn you said a mouthful then Dump, I wonder how many people actually don't know the shit hit the fan yet" said Stewart observing my fire building tepee skills.

"My mom for one" I said with a twinge.

"It will be alright buddy" said Dump patting me kindly on the back.

"Gotta get home" I responded despondently and resumed my arranging some sticks and trash together to light.

"How old is she Dave"? Stewart asked.

"85 and feisty as hell, she's been thru hurricanes she will be ok till I get there" I responded with a nod to myself.

"My Mamma is probably out in her garden cussing about the electricity because the well pump won't work for her to water it" Dump said with a big yawn.

Dump and I had a cup of coffee and Stewart enjoyed his tea as we all contemplated our soon separating of the ways.

"Stewart, it's been nice, we gotta head out. Want me to wash up these cups"? I asked gesturing towards them.

"No, I got the KP today, going to miss you blokes" Stewart replied extending his hand for a shake. "You going to do well Stewart, but don't lose Dumpie's address." I said while getting my gear together.

" Oh I am going to do fine, you mates even made me a proper hotel if your not going to be being taking your mats along with you" Stewart chuckled.

"Mats are free, laying on them costs a dollar" Dump said hugging him around the shoulder with a smile.

He looked at us seriously for a moment and said "Fare thee well".

"And to you, Stewart." I replied and we set off on our journey towards our destinations with the sounds of our temporary host washing up and whistling a tune; and now and then singing a few words, the only ones I could catch though were 'Fare thee Well, Fare the Well...' sending us off.

"Fine fellow" Dump said breaking my thoughts of what lay ahead today.

"That he was, entertaining to say the least" I exclaimed while re-shouldering my pack to the opposite side and already sweating out a few too many beers.

"Looks like some more early starts ahead "said Dump gesturing towards a line of people off in the distance.

10

NOT NECESSARILY THE RIGHT ANSWER

The Group in front of us grew in size as we approached and I could start making out faces. Leading the pack appeared to be a Georgia Highway Patrol Officer in full regalia and every age and race following up his advance.

"Hello" I said as we approached.

"Hi" came back the suspicious response from the LEO.

"How's it looking down the way?" I questioned him surveying the pack of bedraggled strangers. *Something wrong here I thought.* The wayfarers looked more subdued and fearful than I would have expected.

"Pretty bad multi car wreck a mile or so back, it's kind of gory so you might want to change lanes" He said sizing us up through dark sunglasses.

"How about the way you came, any trouble?" he said expectantly, surveying the road we just came down

"Not too many wrecks" I offered.

"Many people?' he countered.

"No, it's pretty deserted most everyone seems to have headed for the nearest exit." I replied eying the group who seemed to be making a point of not paying too much attention to our conversation.

"Any water?' he asked pointedly.

"Uh yea, possibly there's a Perrier truck over in the other far lane" I said diverting him from "Stewart's store".

"Was it open" he asked like I was supposed to produce my driver's license or something.

"Didn't look in it, I don't like the taste of it anyway" I nonchalantly said back.

"Thanks." he replied and then waved his hand like he was leading a wagon train or something and said "Let's move out!!" crossing over the median to the other lane.

Dump was looking puzzled and asked "why did you do that?"

"I got a feeling that gung ho freak might try to say Stewart was looting or something. I am wondering if some of those people following him are prisoners or just refugees putting up with him for protection." I said watching the band of people moving off the road.

"They might just miss Stewart entirely over in that far lane. Did you really see a Perrier Truck over there?' Dump inquired

"Thought I did..." I said grinning and turning to resume our trek once more.

"That looks like a good place to crossover" Dump said gesturing towards a break in the median barrier ahead.

"Yea it does. You know I found 500 bucks under the mattress of the truck I was in yesterday. You need some?" I asked.

"That was a lucky find. Not much to spend it on out here but it might be useful later on. If I need some Ill holler at you" he said while already starting to sweat profusely as the day was warming up. We trudged along occasionally making small talk for the next couple miles and then took the exit ramp to the county road Dump directed me to take.

"You know you might be able to buy a gun of some sort off my cousin, she inherited a bunch of them from her uncle and father awhile back and I don't think she ever did much of anything with them." he advised me.

"Damn, that would be great Dump!" I said looking down the mostly desolate two lane road we had begun traveling on.

"How far do you think we have to go now?" I asked while thinking it was time for another break.

"Maybe 5 or 6 miles as the crow flies." he replied.

"Let's take a break under that billboard and rest for a bit." I said heading off the road and into the weeds.

"We're making better time than I thought today. What's your watch say David?" Dump asked.

"I got 2.30. So maybe we'll get there about 5.30 or 6." I guessed.

"How far is your place from your cousins"? I said while retrieving a bottle of water from my pack and some cheese crackers.

"About 18 miles but it's in the opposite direction from the way you want to go." he replied while cracking open a can of Vienna sausages.

"You want to hang around my cousin's a day or two?" he said between mouthfuls.

"I could use a day to rest up, my feet are pretty sore from these dress shoes" I said dreading the next 5 miles.

"I will hangout with you; I don't have to be right back for any particular reason."

"Good maybe we'll see another beer truck on the way." I joked.

"I imagine my Cousin's got some if my relatives haven't been visiting and drank it all up." Dump said with a sigh as he retied his horseshoe pack.

"Well, let's get 'er done" he said resuming our march under the broiling sun.

11

HOME COMING

"Come on and cut across this field Dave, might save us a mile or two" he said while looking for a good place to hop the barb wire." This acreage borders the cross roads and runs almost up to my cousin's property." Dump said gingerly stepping over a low spot in the rusty barbed-wire fence.

"Looks like who ever own this sold off most of their cattle or changed pastures." I remarked while picking my way across the field.

"Yea appears so, if he sold them, I bet he regrets it now." Dump said avoiding another cow pie in his path.

"There's a fish pond we can visit back in here tomorrow if you want, but I think probably we'd rather just lay around the house recovering." he said navigating our way cross country.

"I like that second option better. Any hope of scrounging up a bicycle from one of your relatives, Dump?" I said wishfully thinking.

"Might be one in my cousin's garage, I'll remember to ask her later." he added.

"We will get back on the road up here; her house is only a few hundred yards away." Dump said gesturing towards a mail box up the road.

We were following the driveway towards a big wooden house with a wrap around porch, when we heard the screen door slam and a stout pudgy women appeared and hollered "Bill, so nice to see ya!" and sort of waddled down hurriedly towards us.

Dump speed up and met her half way and they hugged one another.

"Martha, how are you doing" Dump now called Bill said all smiles and holding her out to arms length.

"Fair to middlin'. Come on to the house." she said as she herded us towards the porch.

"Phew! Bill what you been doing you smell awful". She said turning her nose up.

"Been walking for a couple days", he said plopping down in a chair.

"Why would you need to do that for Bill" she declared with concern.

"Martha this is David" and she and I exchanged pleasantries as I took up residence in another chair next to Dump.

"Told you she wouldn't have noticed" said Dump in my direction.

"Noticed what?" she said crossly eying Dump anew.

"Martha we are in deep shit, the worlds been hit with a thing called EMP and the lights wont be coming on anytime too soon" he declared and proceeded to explain for the next hour just what that meant.

"Well I wondered what knocked the power out a few days ago and I was thinking about going over to your Uncle Jakes and see how they were getting on, but you say no cars will work?" Martha questioned while shuffling for her keys to go out and prove it to herself.

"This is like a bad Sci-Fi movie David" Martha said addressing me skeptically.

"Bill said you were some kind of FEMA folk, are they going to be coming to help out during this?" she demanded to know.

"I explained, not for a long time to come." but left her with a little hope on a possible arrival someday.

"Well, I know you boys is hungry, Bill get your friend something to drink out of that cooler and ill fix up some supper." she said bustling about.

"I had me some frozen milk jugs in the freezer that I put in there and they are not quite melted yet so the drinks will still be cold" she added.

Dump handed me a coke and resumed his seat.

"I got lots of meat in the freezer that will need cooking; you boys want to have a cook out tomorrow?" She inquired

"Sounds good to me" I offered while Dump agreed also.

" I got a bunch of old blankets wrapping up the freezer so I might get a few more days before I need to get it out there" she considered.

"Hey Martha, you got any bicycles in your garage?" Dump asked and I turned to see the response.

"I just got my old one from when I was young, tires probably flat but there's a pump in there" she said pointing in the direction of a barn like building.

"Mind if we have a look" said Dump rising.

"Help yourself, but you won't be able to ride it I don't think Bill, maybe David could. David if you get it going, you mind delivering a message for me about a mile from here?" she said looking at me.

"Be glad too" I said willing to do most anything at this point to get use of a bike.

Bill and I walked over to the shed and opened the door. Assorted tools and junk was everywhere but leaned up against one side was an ugly old purple girls bike complete with banana seat, ape hanger handle bars with streamers, a bell and a white basket in front. The tires were only half flat and after locating the pump we filled them up and wheeled the bike out of the shed.

"Your chariot awaits." Dump said with a flourish towards the frilly machine.

"Well there's no doubt folks will see me coming on that thing." I said mounting it and taking it for an experimental spin around the yard.

Dump was beside himself laughing at me and Martha poked her head out to see what was so funny and stifled a giggle.

"I sure was proud of that thing, back in the day. Hard to imagine me as a girly girl, isn't it, Bill?" she said grinning at Dump.

He dodged the question and asked, "What're we having for dinner?" To which Martha run off a list that would put any country restaurant to shame and said it would be about an hour till we ate.

"Martha, you still got your Daddy's gun collection around here?" he snuck into the conversation.

"Most of it is still back there. I guess you will want to borrow something, Bill, times being what they are. There in the closet in the back bedroom go have a look." she said ducking back in the kitchen.

The closet contained several cased rifles and shotguns and several boxes which could only include pistols and we had a field day snooping around.

"Hey, I got one of those" I said handling a small .380 Sig Sauer 230 stainless pistol. "They used to be the Cadillac of concealed carry in their day." I said dreamily handling it and checking the mechanism to see if it was clear.

"Offer her a hundred bucks for it." Dump said.

"That's a four of five hundred dollar gun, Dump." I objected.

"She don't know values, and besides, where is she going to spend it. Just make the offer." he said settling on a .45 caliber Astra and sticking it in his waistband.

"I get to borrow remember." He smirked and we headed back towards the kitchen.

After a momentary pause contemplating my offer, she said "Sure David I will sell it to you. I got my shotgun and 38 if I need them and there are several other guns around here just collecting dust, so it's a deal." she said to my amazement and Dump's cousin knowing nod.

"Well, thank you very much" I accepted and followed Dump back to the bedroom to get some ammo for it and search around for a holster if one could be found.

The holster I ended up with was a simple affair, just a loop of leather really that slid on your belt. But with my shirttail out the little weapon just disappeared.

"I feel so much better to have a pistol again, Dump." I said.

"Hope you won't have to use it buddy, but I am glad for you too. Makes me fell a lot better, since I won't be there to have your back after tomorrow" he said looking towards the kitchen.

"Yea I am going to miss you my bouncer friend. Hey what kind of message does Martha need me to deliver? I asked

"Martha, David wants to know what kind of message you want him to deliver.

"I want him to stop by Ray's trailer and tell him he ought grab his stuff and move in with me tomorrow. I got chickens, goats and a garden plot that needs tending. Tell him." Martha said while setting various dishes on an already overcrowded table.

Dump waved me closer into a whispered conversation, "She's had her eye set on him for years and now is her chance to reel him in." he sniggered.

"Come on and eat!' Martha called from the dining room and we all settled in on a feast.

"You're cooking with propane.' I said remembering the big silver tanks I had seen in the back.

"Yes, just topped off, last week. I guess I don't have all bad luck after all." she said reloading her plate.

These folks can eat! I was getting tired just watching the two of them go at it. I didn't do too bad myself and had seconds of most everything.

"I will go by Ray's tomorrow morning for you." I said while resting up out on the front porch and looking forward to a softer bed tonight.

"That will be fine, David. He has his own bicycle, by the way, and maybe you can help bring back some things in your little basket." she said picking at me about the garish bike and producing a laugh out of Dump.

"Stranger things have happened." Was all I could come up with, and busied myself studying my remaining brackish tea.

12

RAY`S PLACE

I got on my bike in the morning after receiving directions and cycled down the road to deliver the message. Dump had to be a smart ass and start humming the music from the Wizard of Oz witch riding the bicycle in the storm, as I pushed off.

"You will get yours, Dump." I said as I peddled away.

Riding this bike sure was easier than walking and I was at the old single wide trailer before I knew it. I was getting off the bike and hollering "Ray!" RAY! When a balding older guy in overhauls stepped out of the trailer and looked down at me.

"And who might you be and what does Martha want now?" he asked smiling and reaching out his hand.

"I am David. I take it you recognize the bike?" I answered, laughing as I dismounted.

"That I do. Is she ok?" he asked looking at the spectacle before him.

"Oh, she's fine, she wants you to move in with her and help her with the farm." I said to his watchful twinkling eyes.

"I figured that, took her twenty years to get me in her clutches, but I guess she has got me now. She figured out we had us an EMP event did she?" He said leaning against his porch railing.

"No, me and Dump, err, Bill told her. She was surprised to say the least."

"I didn't figure it out until I noticed those cars stuck in the road up at the intersection. My car wouldn't start and I was riding my bike up to get some help, when I saw them abandoned." He replied

"I'm sure glad you knew what it was, I get tired of explaining it." I said moving onto the porch with him.

"I heard on the news awhile back that NASA predicted such a thing was likely awhile back." he said turning to open his door.

"Come on in. How's that oversized cousin of hers?" he said, while gesturing for me to sit on the couch.

"Big as ever, we've been walking out of Atlanta together for the past two days." I said looking around the trailer.

"Damn, that's a far piece without a vehicle, especially in this heat. I bet Atlanta is looking like a war zone about right now." he said lighting a cigarette and offering me one, which I gladly accepted.

"You want something to drink? I got hot beer and bottled water." he offered.

"I will take the beer, thanks." I said as Ray got up two fetch two cans.

He sat down and handed me mine and I said, "It looks like you are already packed." I said pointing at a backpack and a small suitcase.

"I was going to head to Martha's later on today and tell her the news, pretty much figured she would want me to stay." he said and took a big swig from his beer.

"Nasty stuff, when it's this warm." he said grimacing.

"It grows on ya." I replied taking a gulp out of mine.

"I wasn't going to carry the beer with me this trip. You want to sit around and drink a few before we head out to Martha's?" he asked.

"Sure, Martha is planning a cookout today in order to help use up some of the meat in her freezer. I guess it won't hurt for us to start the party a bit early." I commented.

"Where you from, Dave?' he said rising to go get more beer.

"Montgomery." I replied.

"Hell, that's over 150 miles away, you aren't heading there are you?" he said looking at me in astonishment.

"It will take me awhile to get home, for sure, but I am heading out tomorrow in that direction no matter what. Got kin of my own to see to." I said with some determination.

"You better find you a lawnmower or a horse or something to go all that way," he said pointedly.

"You know where I can find something?" I asked.

"No, but I will think on it some." he said and we went back to our conversation on EMP and what Atlanta might look like by now.

"Ray you want to sell me that backpack when we get to Martha's?" I asked. "That is, if you don't think you will need it." I added seriously.

"I will go you one, better. I got an old Boy Scout pack I will give you and you can use it to carry a couple of six packs back to Martha's with it." He offered with a grin.

"Sounds like a fair deal to me." I agreed. "I got a basket, too, if you think of anything else to tote." I said chuckling about the bike I was forced to ride.

"We shall see." he said and cracked another can open and we settled in to share outlooks on how hard the times were about to be.

"I think winter's going to be the hardest. I don't relish the thought of trying to get what will be needed with just an axe and my own sweat." Ray said looking towards a long cold future.

"I agree, we will lose a lot of the population come fall, as it is. Try to save on that propane she has, as much as you can, and you won't have to chop so much wood." I suggested eying the faded BSA symbol on the old canvas pack Ray had given me.

"Well, Martha is a sensible country girl, but she sure does love to cook. Just might be a bit difficult restraining her from using that oven overly much this summer. " Ray mused.

"Now that outhouses have become fashionable again, she might not be so hard to convince." I said looking out the trailer window.

"Oh, that house has a cistern and a septic tank, I will rig something so we can keep the indoor plumbing." he declared.

"Well, you about ready to get going?" I asked, watching as Ray loaded two six-packs into what was soon to b e my bag.

"Just need to load up and lock up and we can go." said Ray, rising to his feet.

"I figure chainsaws will most likely work, until the gas goes bad." I interjected eying Ray's boat parked off to the side. "You got any Stabil gasoline additive?" I inquired.

"Sure, do. Good idea." He said heading towards his storage shed.

"Add it to my basket." I offered with a smile.

13

THE GREAT SMOKE OUT

Ray and I peddled up to Martha's drive way sweating out our previously consumed adult libations. We could see Dump laboring over the barbeque pit and it looked like he had a good fire going.

"Hi, Ray! "Dump hollered across the yard. "Long times no see!" he said enthusiastically in our direction, then looking towards the house expectantly.

The screen door slowly opened and out waltzed Martha in what might have been what they call a sun dress or a circus tent. I couldn't tell which. She evidently had taken the time to put some war paint on, however, and demurely called out a "Hi Ray. Nice of you to drop by." and "Thanks, Dave, now Ray and I need to talk." and locked elbows with him guiding him towards the house, leaving a flabbergasted Dump Truck and Dave in her wake to tend to other business.

"Oh, God he is in for it now." Dump said happily, directing me towards the grill.

"Did they used to be an item, Dump?" I asked inspecting his roaring blaze that would be reduced to good hardwood coals eventually.

"They grew up together and until she added a hundred pounds or so, used to occasionally date." he said poking at the fire with a hoe.

"She has always had a thing for him though, and been trying to doll up since you left hours ago. What have you been doing anyway, I was starting to get worried?" he asked adjusting his new found pistol.

"Well, it's Rays beer, but seeing how he is indisposed, I guess is ok to offer you one." delving into my pack.

"She got out a half gallon of Jack from somewhere she has been saving for just this sort of occasion." Dump said, smirking about his cousin and her intended Beau as usual. "I don't think he will mind if we drink up his beer." he said raking the coals down more to his liking.

"That's a damn huge fire Dump, you been taking lessons from Stewart?" I asked, opening up a beer of my own.

"Well, she has got over a side of beef in that freezer, plus some pork, she said she could can some, if I got it mostly done." he said inquisitively towards me seeking some suggestions.

"We need to smoke some of it and make some jerky or pemmican out of it then, if you got that much." I said pondering.

"I am up on jerky, but what's pemmican?" Dump replied sucking the bottom out of his beer.

"It's basically preserving meat by rendering lard or tallow." I offered. "The pioneers got it from the Indians and the meat lasts forever. You mix clear fat with pulverized meat and berries and/or nuts and seal it up in something." I explained.

"Well, we got about 10 lbs of frozen pecans and there are blackberries in season growing around here." he said looking around.

"Perfect, I can make us some trail rations and have a bunch left over. You got any old pipe around here, Dump?" I said contemplating building a smoker and looking towards the jumble of goods I had seen in the garage previously.

"I saw some bits and pieces earlier. What do you need?" he said and heading off towards the shed.

"They can make Jerky in the oven for now, but since you got the makings of a smoker and that fire producing some great coals: let's dig us a pit and find a tarp to pipe some of that smoke into." I suggested.

"Hell, let's move the whole freezer out here and make one out of that." Dump suggested catching onto the idea.

"Beats digging any day." I said following his lead and we began our construction.

Occasional raised voices drifted out from the main house as Dump and I labored over our task.

"Seems he is not in complete agreement with us." Dump said chuckling, while we fitted the pipe to our improvised smoker.

"Could be he don't like the size of his corral." I said while shuddering at what Martha might be demanding of him.

"Oh, they will sort it out, they actually love and need each other." he said finishing up a sheet metal flange with a ball peen hammer.

"Look, the love birds are coming out to join us." he spoke while finding something else to pretend he had his attention on.

"Bill? How's that fire coming, and what on earth is that creation." she declared surveying our handiwork.

"It's a smoker." Dump declared, as our audience took in the mangled looking chest freezer we had carried out from the back porch.

"Now, that's slick." said Ray, while distancing himself from his nemeses and asked, "How's it work?" feigning interest in the contraption to avoid the dagger-like, but wistful stares coming from Martha.

We explained the process of getting cooler smoke from our fire, while Martha sipped what appeared to be most likely a Jack and coke.

" Hell, that's at least 3 months worth of food you guys are creating there." he said, allowing Martha to slip up to him and reservedly taking claim to her by attempting to encircle her waist with his arm.

"Martha and I have agreed to marry." he said dejectedly, "Since you are the only official, other than God, will you seal the marriage, David?"

I was thunderstruck, as was Dump. "I am not any kind of official Ray. I didn't even have a job a few days ago." I adamantly said.

"You're what we got and I have agreed. Do a ceremony Dave and Bill, you witness." he forlornly said.

"Are you serious?" I asked and looked imploringly into each of their eyes.

"Yes, we are Dave." said Martha back resolutely.

"Dump. Go find a Bible." I said near-speechlessly, as he stared open-mouthed at both of them.

"We got to do this right." I said searching for words, while Martha looked to be blushing or getting ready to tell me to hurry up.

Old Truck was still dumbfounded and hadn't moved yet.

"There's one on the nightstand." she said pushing him in the direction of the house.

"Ya'll are sure about this?" I inquired, as Dump went on his mission and I looked closely at them again.

"We have agreed." Martha said pointedly, as Dump Truck trotted back with Bible in hand, mission complete.

"Cross your hands on the Bible. Do you, Ray, promise to love and cherish Martha till death do you part?"

A weak, "Yes," came from Ray.

"And, do you, Martha, promise to love and to hold Ray till death do you part?"

To which Martha sang out, "YES, I do."

"By the powers invested in me, by you and before our Lord, I declare you Man and Wife." I said feeling very peculiar in this role.

"Kiss your Bride, Ray." I finished saying and surprisingly he did and did so with gusto.

"I heard there was some Jack around here." I said laughing. "Every marriage needs a toast." I said in anticipation of being able to partake.

"I will go get it." Martha said with a lot of color in her cheeks that did not belong to the weather or possible imbibing before the event.

"Back in a minute." she said flouncing towards the house.

"Well, you old rascal, you took the big jump, didn't you." said Dump extending his hand towards Ray.

"She didn't give me a lot of choices, Bill." he said returning the handshake. "But I will be good." he assured my concerned friend.

"Who is that?" I asked, gesturing towards a stranger moving slowly down the road.

"Looks like Philburn Stiles." declared Ray, moving towards the man with some recognition and concern.

"That's who it is, alright." said Dump scrutinizing the newcomer.

"Hey Stiles, you need some help? Ray called while continuing to walk faster towards the zombie-like figure and Dump and I hurriedly tried to catch up.

"I need some water," the old man croaked as Ray put an arm out to steady him.

"Sure Phil, let me just help you over to this shade tree. Bill, go get some water for him, please." Ray said letting the gray faced man down gently next to an old oak.

Dump returned from getting the water and handed it to Stiles, who greedily began guzzling it down.

"Easy there, Stiles. Don't make yourself sick." Ray said touching the man on the shoulder.

"Ok." Phil said, slowing his efforts and looking like a deflated bag of bones.

Martha wandered up then, looking like a concerned mother hen.

"Philburn, you look all done in, what's done happened?" she clucked worriedly looking down at him.

"Let me catch my breath and I will tell you all about it" he wheezed out, while mopping the sweat off his forehead with a shirt sleeve.

"Bill, go get Phil a towel, if you would." Martha said while still looking anxiously at the old man.

"I will be alright in a bit; I am just wore slam out." Phil said, while thanking Dump for the towel and sitting up a little straighter, though he was still looking deathly pale.

"Dump, we need to tend that smoker and make sure it's not getting too hot." I said looking towards it.

"Martha and I can see to Philburn. You two go do what you need to do. You think you can make up to the porch?" Ray said and extending a hand to the man to give him some help up.

"Might be a bit cooler up there, at that." Phil said, as he grunted wearily, while grabbing on to Ray's proffered hand with both of his and pulling himself up.

Dump and I checked the fire and busied ourselves seasoning the meat to go on the grill and discussed various recipes to season the jerky to be going into the oven later on in the day.

"Dump. Who is that guy? He was looking pretty peeked?" I said gesturing towards the porch.

"That's one of the bigger local landowners and a real estate agent. He is also somewhat of a skin flint, if you know what I mean." Dump said, while creating some kind of mystery rub to go on the lesser cuts of meat from the side of beef we were trying to contend with.

"We don't have time to do it today, but let me tell you a trick to tenderize those pieces with. You see Chinese restaurants buy those cheaper cuts often times to make up a dish and they coat them with baking soda for about 24hours. As long as you're sure to wash the baking soda off good before you cook it, it does a great job of tenderizing or use it on deer to remove some of that wild taste." I explained. "Neat, I will try that some day. Let me cover this meat up and we will go hear Phil burns story." he said while grabbing a roll of foil.

14

PHILBURN'S FOLLY

Dump and I wandered up to the expansive covered porch and sat down. I noticed Phil was starting to get a little color back in his cheeks, but still looked the worse for wear.

"Phil, do you need to take an aspirin?" I inquired.

"I got some heart pills, I take. But thanks for thinking about it." Phil replied.

"This is David," Ray said to Phil, who was still barely moving.

"Pleasure, David, wish I could of met you on a better day." he sighed.

"Me, too," I replied looking towards Ray and Martha inquiringly.

"Phil's been telling us how bad Newnan is getting, go ahead with your story Phil." he said while turning to Martha.

"Martha get Bill and David a drink, we haven't had our toast yet." Ray said warily to his new spouse.

"Completely slipped my mind in the confusion." she said rising and opening the screen door to go into the house.

"What are you toasting, Ray?" Phil said adjusting himself straighter in his chair.

"Martha and me just got hitched." he said sheepishly.

"I'll be damned! When was the wedding? I didn't hear anything about it." Phil responded with interest.

"About 5 minutes, before you fell out on the front lawn. I will tell you about that later, you were telling us that there was something we needed to know." he said looking worriedly at Phil.

"You got a plague of locusts heading your way, Ray." and he settled back to tell his story, as Martha came back and handed Dump and I our drinks.

"You don't get one until you looking better, Phil." she said apologetically, but firmly.

"I don't touch the stuff usually, but I will help celebrate your occasion later. Congratulations, by the way!" he said trying to show more enthusiasm than he felt.

"Well, getting back to my story. I was sitting in Susie's Drive in on the outskirts of town, when this shit hit. At first, we all thought it was a power outage, until the cars passing along the road out front started to just slow down and stop. There were folks breaking down everywhere and that Georgia power boy, Silas, said something about EMP to who ever was listening. And we all asked a question or two watching the shocked folks get out their cars in wonderment and start to head towards the diner.' He stated morosely while rocking back in his chair and looking towards Martha.

"Darling, I might just need that drink now please, I will be ok." he reassured.

"Well, if you can handle it, Ill get it." she said still looking at him suspiciously, but rising to go mix him one.

"Well, folks kept coming and coming, until the place was filled up and people were just milling around in the parking lot. Nobody knew what to do and the owner Suzie was freaking out, as people started demanding water and the taps weren't working." He paused to take his drink from Martha and then resumed his story.

" It was bedlam, I tell you, inside of there with people packing in like sardines and talking all at once, so I thought I best get out of there, before it got out of hand." he reminisced wincingly.

"How many people, you figure Phil?" Dump asked looking worried.

"When I left that parking lot there must have been at least a 150 people and more walking towards it." he thoughtfully considered.

"That's what I wanted to warn you about. I been smelling that Barbeque you been making for the last two miles." he said seriously looking around at all our faces.

"I was on the outskirts of Newnan, mind you, no telling how many people will be coming up that exit from the interstate and joining that horde of folks. You guys are off the main drag, but I can't imagine what all those people are going to do for food and drink." he said ominously, letting the thought of a mass of refugees descending on our cook out sink in.

Martha started looking like she was going to lose her composure and cast a frightened look towards the road before speaking.

"David, you know about mobs and such, what do we do." she said imploringly and everyone put me on the spot staring in my direction.

Shit, I ain't been trained for this I thought. While I tried to carefully frame an answer for my attentive hosts.

"First thing we do is load what ever long arms we got and keep them handy. Most people will leave you alone by just seeing you armed. We don't have any idea how many folks will come this way, but if it's small groups we help who we can, but be adamant about them having to keep moving on." I said looking for anyone coming up either side of the road.

"What about that smoker, David? Should we put it out?" Dump said eying the outdoor kitchen we had set up.

"Too late for that, we got at least six more hours of burn time needed to finish what we started and folks won't be so desperate yet, that they'd try to force an issue, if we look armed to the teeth." I said decidedly.

"I can shoot, if you need me to." Phil said dejectedly as he realized he wasn't going to be able to just rest today.

"Let's just get prepared for the worst, and hope for the best. Dumps, get those guns out and I will bike up the road and do a little recon to see if I can anticipate just what we might be in for." I said rising to my feet.

"I am on it." Dump said heading in to the house.

"What should we be doing while you are gone?" Ray said accepting, but not really trusting my judgment yet.

"Help Dump load, and make up some signs on cardboard or something to say 'no trespassing', 'move on' etc. Philburn can keep watch, if he is feeling up to it. Dump needs to watch the fire and kind of play roving guard and occasionally look for me to be coming back, I shouldn't be long." I said getting ready to mount that stupid looking bike.

"You can borrow mine to do that." Ray said to my instant relief.

"It will be just fine, Martha." I said consolingly and mounting Ray's bicycle and heading out down the driveway.

"Be careful!" she cried to my departure.

"I must have been a danged fool to walk all that way in my condition, but I didn't know what else to do." Phil said to Dump, who was handing him a shotgun and watching my departure.

"Sounds like you had no choice, to me." Dump said, uncasing a lever action 30-30 and reaching towards his back pocket for a box of ammo to go with it.

"Damn, there is a friggin' arsenal in that closet!" Ray said carrying out two rifle cases and a pistol box.

Martha interjected into the men's conversation and admiration of the weapons with, "What kind of signs did David say to make?" she admonished, as if to say nobody should get trigger happy.

"He said something about just getting the message across that people should keep moving on by this place." Phil offered.

"Let's put up a big sheet with skull and crossbones on it." Dump suggested looking wicked.

"That's not what he meant, he said we should help small groups, but be prepared for repelling mobs." Martha scolded.

"That would repel me..." Dump started to say, before Martha and Ray looked at him pointedly.

"I better go check that fire." Dump said picking up a Marlin 30-30.

"You do that, and don't forget to look for Dave coming back, in case he needs you." Martha said, while feeling Phil's forehead like she was doing some kind of good in this hundred degree weather.

A belligerent, but chastised, Dump Truck wandered back to his cooking efforts and resumed the chore of leveling the coals. Meantime, Ray talked to Phil about the impromptu wedding and his and Martha's plans to team up and get through this radical change in living conditions.

"Philburn, you still got horses over at your place?" Ray asked contemplating a lead into a conversation where he might just be able to have the upper hand with this old horse trader, for a change.

"I got a couple of old retired nags, but I just got done selling off most of my stock. Wish I hadn't, we got a use for them now don't we." He said with the same old dollar signs in his eyes Ray was used too from past dealings with the old miser.

"You still got any of those old tractors you used to collect?" Ray said setting the old negotiator up for a fall.

He doesn't really collect them he just buys up old pieces of shit and gets them barely running to sell to someone as "Antique" when he can get away with it, Ray thought to himself.

"Oh, I got a couple, I been restoring, you seen that rare one I got out on the road in front of my place with the for sale sign on it?" His eyes sparkling as his nose smelled new money out of trash. "Think it can still run, now do you, after what just happened?" Phil shrewdly inquired.

"It might still work, you referring to that old Hoyt Clagwell looking thing you probably got off Mr. Haney on Green Acres?" Ray said drawing his victim in and working on driving down the price.

"Hey, that's a crank start 1950 Massey Ferguson; they don't make them like that anymore!" Phil objected.

"They don't make them like that any more for a reason!" looking at his prey wolfishly and then carrying on.

"Did that old rust bucket run when you parked it to the side of the road?" Ray said mentally licking his chops.

" Now, see here, that's a valuable antique, I admit its condition needs some paint, but I ain't taking less than $900 for it as is and it will crank." Phil huffed.

"How are you going to get home Phil, you thought about that yet?" Making the old reprobate realize he had been had, hook line and sinker.

"What are you saying, Ray?" Phil said irately.

"I am saying I got a proposition for you that you can't refuse." and commenced to tell him the deal I had struck to get that god awful bike and that I might just be willing to ride him home on it, if I got a tractor out of the deal, and sat back smugly knowing he had the winning hand.

"Shit, you a hard trader Ray, there's no way I can make it back the 7 miles to my place by foot after the ordeal I done been through." He said with lighting bolts coming out of his old grey blue eyes.

"I ain't done with you, yet." Ray said hitching his fingers under the straps of his overalls and toying with his quarry.

" You going to get Davies's bike out of the deal and we ain't traded for that yet, nor the cost of your upkeep while residing on my place, oops, our place." casting a glance at an intrigued, but correcting Martha.

"You're gouging me, going too far." Philburn said, apparently outraged, while trying to direct the conversation back towards a more palatable deal for himself.

"You have been screwing every one around here for years." Martha looked at him intently. "'Fair will be fair', as we see it or move on." she said reproachfully and looking pointedly towards the road.

"Ok, name your terms." a defeated Phil said.

Ray started counting on his fingers, "For a ride home, David gets the tractor and it better run." he said looking at the misbegotten old man.

"It does, but uses oil." Phil offered a bit cowed.

"Two," Ray ticked off on his fingers, remembering how many times this old codger had got him on a deal or a loan payment. "My time or my money is not free, as you have been known to say so many times, we pay for convenience or we can go to the bank, as you used to like to remind me regarding interest rates or repayment schedules." He spoke towards a thoroughly trapped loan shark and enjoying every minute of it.

A long pause occurred, as the two eyed each other, then Philburn busted out laughing and dug for his wallet saying, "Ok, now how much for the bike." and grinning at Martha.

Dump had wandered back by now and had heard bits and pieces of the conversation. Phil noticed him coming up in back of him and said, "Damn Ray, you didn't need to call the bouncer, I was agreeing." he said jovially and extending his aged hand towards Truck.

"What did I miss?' Dump asked softly, taking the man's hand and looking towards Martha and Ray for explanations.

"Your friend might be riding home on a tractor, if this scalawag is telling me the truth." Ray said leaning back in his chair and sharing a moment of mutual respect with what once was a feared bill collector.

"Oh, she runs, I guarantee that, or did. I don't really understand how the Sun can affect technology yet, but you got my word that thing can drive down the road or did before this." He said towards Ray, who was looking bemused.

"Ok, for bike rental or sale, you need to lend me a horse, so I can come to help you put in a crop with one of those other tractors, when I get around to peddling my way down there to see about you." Ray offered.

"You are going to do that for us? As miserable as I have been?" Phil said, doing a bit of self reflection." Bless you!" he said reaching slowly towards Ray.

"Times have changed, we all got to paddle the same canoe now." he said now and looking off worriedly in the direction I had traveled.

15

LAWYERS, GUNS AND MONEY

This road looks pretty clear I thought, as I pumped the pedals along towards Newnan. *I wonder what's in back of me, people are either coming towards or away from a destination,* I was thinking, as I saw my first group of travelers. A man had his suit coat slung over his shoulder and was leading, what I guessed was his family of a wife and two kids, down the road. He looked up at me as I was coasting down the hill towards them.

"Got a minute?" I asked while applying the coaster brake and slowing in their direction.

"Where you coming from?" the man replied, obviously put off about my strange presence on this bicycle and condition of my modified suit.

"Just checking on neighbors." I replied, trying to act like I belonged there. "Want to share some water?" I said producing a 2 liter from my white floral emblazoned wicker basket.

"Awful kind of you." He replied, still trying to get an understanding of the odd spectacle before him, as his wife reached around and gathered up the kids and moved closer to him.

"Dustin Majors." he said offering his hand and taking the bottle from me.

"David Dupree." I said looking down the road and returning the handshake.

"You got many Folks in back of you?" I attempted cheerily, so his wife would release her charges.

"What do you want?" he said making an obvious attempt at letting me see his shoulder holster and what might have been a Glock residing in it.

"Not a thing, I was just being civil." I somewhat snarled back warningly, thinking I could beat him to the draw, if it went there.

"Hey, we're sorry." said the woman releasing her kids and stepping forward with a cautionary hand on the man.

"It's been a bad day, I am Angela and this is Steve and Julie." she said exposing the children.

"I agree, I just thought you looked thirsty and I wanted a bit of news." I said keeping my eyes on the man, but physically relaxing and acknowledging the wee ones.

"My bad, friend, it's a zoo back there and I am a bit jumpy after last night." he said, still curious as to why I was not put off by the flash of his piece.

"What happened last night?" I said relaxing and watching them pass around the bottle of water.

"Damned group of punks wanted to fuck with us in the middle of the night, while we were trying to sleep. I almost capped one!" He said flashing his pistol again.

"Dustin! Watch the language!" his wife said, nudging him and drawing the kids nearer, like that was supposed to keep them from hearing.

I attempted to get the conversation on a more positive track and said, "Glad you didn't have to, but you run them off anyways." I offered.

"Oh, yeah, they took off like scalded dogs, when I fired a round off in the air." He declared proudly and the wife and kids shuddered.

"So, have you seen a lot of travelers today?" I allowed scanning the road for others.

"We decided to take the road less traveled, but I am not sure exactly where this ends up, we were going to her mom's at Fullers cross roads, which is in this general direction." he said, wishing I would supply him more information.

"When you get to your second set of crossroads, that's it. Only about two more miles ahead."

"Hey, thanks I should recognize which way at the intersection." said Dustin.

Good, they are not even going past Martha's I thought.
"How did you come to get stuck in the monkey suit on this fine day," I said gesturing towards my own dress pants and shoes.

"I am a lawyer, it's a dress code thing." he said, as if I was going to automatically start telling Lawyer jokes, which I got to admit, I did consider.

"Well, good luck to you folks and stay safe, I got some more rounds to make." I said and began peddling away.

"Bye, David." they all chorused.

What the hell, they're probably armed for bear, too, by now. I thought when I turned off the road and into the driveway to signs literally everywhere. I almost fell over laughing at one: ***IF YOU LOOKING FOR TROUBLE KEEP MOVING ON***

16

A WONDERFUL SOLUTION

"Hey, Dumpie!" I said as I wheeled around the bush he was attempting to hide behind and casually lowering his Marlin as he recognized me, or more probably, my conveyance.

"How's, the road look?" he said with anticipation.

"Nobody seems to be using it, thank the heavens." I said looking around.

"You kind of overdid it on the signs, didn't you?" I said observing a "Burma shave" line that extended in both directions.

"That was Martha." Dump said aggravated.

"She made us make and situate every one of those, because she thought that's what you wanted, Dave." he declared, like I had something to do with the printing press Martha had produced.

"What's Phil up to, he recovering?" I asked as I started up the driveway.

"He is back In Korea." Dump considered and draining the last of a hot beer. "Ray found him an old M1 A1 rifle and he is back in the zone giving advice, although he was a paymaster, not a foot soldier." he said for update, as to what had transpired after I left,

"Hi, looks like Martha is keeping you busy." I observed.

"Shit, she has been a whirl of activity since you left David, had me spreading mustard on sandwiches for people I don't even know" Phil said resentfully to Martha's returning glare..

"Hey Dupree, I cut a deal for you." Ray said grinning.

"You are going to ride Papa Stiles back home on your bike." said Ray carrying on knowingly.

"Do what?' I said trying to imagine that crazy picture.

"It's a fair trade." Martha offered before giving Ray a chance to explain the convoluted deal that was made previously

"I wouldn't mind doing it a bit under those conditions." I carefully said.

Phil looked up at me and said, "You going to be able to peddle me all that ways, Dave?"

"Hell, I would find a way to carry you all the way, for the loan of that tractor." I replied grabbing one Martha's hefty sandwiches.

"Your buddy is a tough negotiator." Phil said smiling at a grinning Ray.

"Appears to be." I acknowledged. "You going to be all right to travel tomorrow, Phil"? I said, concerned about his health.

"As well as I will ever be. I might slow you down some, though. I will need to take several breaks. "He replied wearily.

"No problem, we will take as many breaks as you need." I said settling back in the chair and thinking about tomorrow's road trip.

"Looks like you get your scout pack back, Ray. I don't think I could wear it without overcrowding Phil on that shortened banana seat." I contemplated.

"I got an old Boy scout pack I will give you when I get to the house. And yeah, you can have it for free before any one asks." he said smiling at everyone.

17

YOU GOT A TICKET TO RIDE

"Dump, I am going to miss you buddy." I said looking at my trail companion and loading some water bottles into the flowery basket.

"I am going to miss you too, now we got our own personal adventures starting again my friend. I am going to hang out here for a few days and make some plans." He said leaning against the porch railing.

Martha came out from the kitchen and said, "I made you and Phil lunches and I got some beef jerky you need to find room for." she said handing me two bags.

"I appreciate all the hospitality, Martha. Good luck Ray." I said hugging Martha and shaking Ray's hand.

"Climb on, Phil, lets get this road trip started." I declared.

"Phil, I will be down your way in a few days to check on you and figure out what we need to do about the gardens." Ray said.

"I will see you then, and I sure do appreciate it." Phil replied warmly.

I said, "Hang on Phil." and we were off with a chorus of good byes ringing in the background.

We didn't talk much first mile or so, as Phil was trying to stay balanced and hanging on for dear life, every time I tried to share the seat with him. I noticed a yappy little dog starting to approach us and stopped the bike, so it didn't start try to nip at our heels and hollered at it to go home, while chucking a small pebble at it.

"Phil, dogs on these country roads don't mix with bicycles to good, hang on second I am going to get something off that car ahead." I told him.

"Antenna?" he questioned.

"No, something stouter, a dip stick." I said wheeling over to the vehicle.

"That will make good critter getter." he said handling the flattened steel stick.

"Put it under the rope on my pack and you or I either one can grab it." I said turning around some so he had access and then remounting the bike.

We rode on pretty uneventfully the next few miles and with an occasional water break, Phil was holding up well.

"You want a lunch break or you want to keep on?" I asked him over my shoulder.

"Might as well go on, we only got a few miles left." he said sweating profusely, but not that chalky grey he was yesterday.

I thought how glad I was that we would make it without a medical emergency or God forbid the old guy dying on me. My legs were tired, but this sure does beat walking and at least there is a bit of breeze today.

We arrived at his home a lot sooner than I expected and Phil directed me into his long winding drive way. *This guy sure has a bunch of land* I thought as we came up to a big white antebellum looking house.

"That's your tractor over in the corner of the field." he said pointing a few hundred yards away. *Didn't look to bad at this distance, though it was hard to tell at this distance I thought.*

"Come on in and we will rest a bit before you go play with it" he said unlocking his front door.

"I got lots of can goods, but we can see if anything is still good enough to eat in the freezer, too. I assume your going to stay for supper and maybe spend the night?" He inquired hopeful of the company.

"I would appreciate that, Phil. I don't know these roads around here and I don't relish the thought of driving them at night. Does that tractor have headlights?" I said wondering what I could do if it didn't.

"It's got them, but I don't know if they work or not. I never tried them to be honest. Let's go see if that thing even cranks and you can explain to me on the way, why some things might work when most things don't." he said while looking into a soggy freezer.

"This meat on the bottom is still a bit frozen, how about grilling us a T bone steak for dinner, Dave?"

"Great! Let's go see about that tractor first." I said very curious about what condition it was actually in after hearing Phil and Ray go at it about its appearance and mechanics.

Phil I set off across the field and the closer we got, I saw it didn't really look all that bad.

"Now she uses a bit of oil, but if you keep an eye on it you shouldn't have any problems. She is a little cantankerous to start so don't be put off if it don't fire up on the first few tries." He said, climbing up into the seat and I went around front to crank it.

"Now I know you done this before, but just have a listen to me for a minute, Dave." he said advancing the throttle a couple notches and turning on the gas.

Phil said "If the tractor is properly tuned, hand cranking is a relatively simple process. Two major things to look out for: NEVER, EVER wrap your thumb around the crank. Cup your hand and lay your thumb along side the crank handle. If, for some reason, she kicks back (backfires) and the crank doesn't disengage, you won't spend an hour looking all over the yard for your thumb. For the same reason, crank only on the UPSTROKE. Pushing down on the crank is a good way to get your elbow permanently embedded in your ear."

"All great advice, Phil." I replied.

The process on these things is something like this.
   1. Turn on the gas
2. Advance the throttle a couple of notches
3. Double check to make sure it's in neutral
4. Set the spark advance about half way
5. Set the choke

6. Engage the crank onto the crankshaft pins and turn SLOWLY until you are at or near the bottom of the stroke and you hear the impulse on the mag click.

7. Pull up sharply to the top of the stroke and let go of the crank.

8. Repeat 6 and 7 until it starts.

Well I repeated six and seven about 5 times and then VROOOM! It started! I hopped up on the side of Phil and off we went laughing back towards the house.

"Hey Phil where do you want Martha's bike parked?" I asked moving it out of the way.

"I ought to mount the damn thing over the fireplace for a conversation piece, but its just plain too ugly to look at." He laughed and added, "Just leave it sit there. I will make Ray do something with it later."

"I could have strapped it onto the front of the tractor as a hood ornament, if Ray hadn't of already traded it to you." I joked back.

"You want it, you can have it." Phil said grimacing.

I thought about it for a moment and said, "No I think its time me and that bike parted ways. I sure am glad I don't have to try to ride to Montgomery on that thing." I said with a sigh of relief.

"You want a drink Dave? Seems we both got a lot to celebrate and be thankful for. I got a bottle of Gentleman Jack I keep for such occasions." He said heading towards the house.

We got our drinks and headed out to the back porch of the house and I took in the sight of a huge barn and several horses in the back pasture.

"After dinner I will show you the Barn and my other tractors" he said settling into a lounge chair.

"I will finish this drink and start the fire. Where's the grill?"

"It's over there," he said motioning off to the side of the courtyard. "But it's the gas kind, so no need to worry with it for awhile."

"You know Phil, it won't be long until the hunters are out in force, you might want to keep them horses closer in." I said watching them serenely wandering in the distance.

"I need to think about other security, too." he said thoughtfully sipping his drink. "Now that I know old tractors and some older cars with points and carbs will run, I am going to round me up some live-in farm help to help take care of things." he said while reaching for my glass. "Let me get you another." turning to go in the house, while I was telling him I'd forgotten to check the tractor's head lights and headed around front.

I turned them on and they worked just fine, so I went back to my chair and Phil and I talked long into the night.

18

ON THE ROAD AGAIN

I fired up the old tractor and arranged the pack that Phil gave me and followed him out of the driveway. Phil had saddled one of his horses and was going to go check on a neighbor. We progressed as far as his turn off, and then we waved goodbye to each other, and I putt-putted on down the road towards home.

I figured I could do about 15 miles an hour and not stress out this old beast too badly. *Let's see, I calculated, that should put me at the city limits in about 10 hour's if I got back on the interstate somewhere. Wow! That's a hell of a difference from the weeks it would have taken me walking or even riding that stupid bike.*

I think I will stay back roads, as much as I can, and pick some obscure exit to get back on the interstate. I sure didn't relish the thought of seeing mobs of refugees wanting to get a hold of my tractor. I rode on for a while avoiding cars and trucks in the road and only occasionally seeing a homeowner who waved for my attention, but I just kept on going by as fast as the tractor would let me.

Hell, it looks like its going to rain soon; I hope it doesn't get too bad. All I got for protection is one of those disposable plastic paint tarps and the canvas one I used for my pack earlier if I needed some shelter. I better stop and cut a hole in the plastic one for my head to fit through soon, I thought as thunder started to rumble.

I better check the oil in this thing, too, I thought. I am glad Phil supplied me with a gas can and a laundry bag full of oil bottles or this trip might've started out twice as long. I can just see me having to rob cars for oil or gas, well I would have to get some more gas eventually, but siphoning doesn't take long.

I can't get that opening song from Green Acres TV show out of my head. I chuckled to my self thinking, *how surprised my mom's going to be seeing me ride up on this thing, if it makes it. It will make it, think positive.* I reminded myself.

I made a little pit stop on a deserted stretch of road and rigged me a poncho, after I put gas and oil into the tractor.

Oh hell, it's starting to drizzle, come on rain just hold off a bit longer, I was hoping or I was going to get drenched.

The rain held off for about an hour or so and then started intermittently coming down. *Well, at least it's not storming.* I allowed while trying to keep the rain out of my eyes. I hadn't seen anywhere to get under cover, so I might as well just grin and bear it. *You know this rain might help me out, if I got back on the interstate, everybody would be seeking shelter in cars and not be all in the road* I figured.

I started towards the interstate and came on at an exit with very few stores. I didn't see any signs of life around and the buildings didn't look like they had been broken into yet.

This was always a desolate stretch of highway with few exits and mostly wooded terrain. There were relatively few cars on the road, but I saw an occasional face peering out the window watching my passing in a moderate rain. I saw one, I think prepper, taking refuge from the rain at an underpass with a military looking backpack and a bicycle heading towards Atlanta or one of its surrounding towns. Guy was pretty cool as I gunned it and came whizzing by. He held up his hand and gave me a thumbs up which I happily returned.

What do we have here?" I wondered a few miles later, while slowing the tractor and looking ahead at a RV on the road shoulder with its awning out.

104

An elderly couple was sitting outside under the tarp in lawn chairs and waved to me. I slowed down and stopped the tractor in front of the vehicle and we exchanged hellos.

"Mind if I get out of the rain for a bit?" I asked.

"Sure. I will get you a chair." the man said.

"My name's Sara, that's my husband, John." she said motioning to him coming out the door of the RV with another folding chair.

"I am David." I replied John extended his hand to shake it but I said "I am pretty wet" he said he understood and to have seat.

"I like your chariot there." John said eying my rusty heap.

"So far it's getting me where I am going and I am grateful for it." I replied pulling off my rain sheet. "I see you folks are making the best of it." I said not knowing where to start.

"We might as well, Sara and I are not going anywhere, so this is now home." he responded giving his wife's hand a squeeze.

"Well, at least you got a nice pond over there to look at." I said gazing out into a field.

"Yes, that's something to be thankful for." Sarah said looking at the fairly large body of water. "We haven't figured out if it belongs to a farm or not yet, but will check it out in a few days."

"Do you think it has any fish in it, Dave?" John asked.

"Most likely does, probably bream and bass." I considered.

"Sara and I do like to fish." John responded happily.

"Well, there you go; a ready made vacation spot." I said trying to stay on a positive note.

"We had a guy come by on a bike yesterday that said he thought that property might have several ponds on it." Sara said snuggling closer to John.

"That's not uncommon around here; a lot of big landowners stock them." I informed them.

The rain had started to let up and we continued to make small talk for a bit. I had about 70 more miles to go and was itching to get home, but felt I might need to stick around here for awhile and maybe share some useful information and a bit of food.

"I got to be moving along shortly, but I have some food with me and I would like share, if you would care to have a road side picnic with me" I offered.

"How nice." Sarah said looking towards John for approval. "We would love to." she said accepting my invitation.

"Well, let me get some stuff off my tractor, Montgomery can wait another hour or so." and proceeded to get what I had intended to be sharing.

19

Stranded On The Side Of The Road

David sat back and listened to the Cicadas sing as dusk fell on the highway.

"John, you know that you might be signing your own death warrant staying out here." I whispered now that Sarah had gone inside to put up the few cans of tuna and jerky I was leaving with my adopted couple.

John considered for a small pause and replied, "We've lived a good life Dave, we can meet our Maker anytime now without regrets, but don't scare Sarah, and she is ok right now with our lot." he said rheumy eyed

"I don't intend to." David said weighing his options. "This is a great place for a young man to make it, but you aren't a young man." I reminded him and rose to extend my hand to Sarah making her way out the door of the RV.

"Thank you, David. Nice to see a man with some manners." Sarah said casually settling down next to John.

John appeared a bit flustered about our previous secret conversation and his wife of many years picked up on it quick.

"Did I interrupt something?" she said looking concerned in John's direction?

"Oh not really, Dave here was telling me I needed to remember some old skills I'd forgot about food gathering is all." He said pointedly at me.

"Johns always been a good provider, David, no worries here" she said confidently patting her hubby.

"What concerns you, David that upset him?" she said searching both our faces for emotions.

"Oh nothing, we were arguing about the finer points of fishing, as men folk do." trying to put the ball back in his court, I said shrugging off her concerns.

"You men. Always got to be bigger or the best." she said with some humor.

"David, he knows his way around a fishing hole and might just give you a run for your money." She jibed while happily caressing John's hand.

"I bet he could." I responded jovially to Sara and saw that John settled back in his chair relaxing, while patting Sara for the compliment.

I had just drove 75 miles on a tractor after walking at least 35, by the time I happened on this loving couple. Something in me didn't want to desert them on the side of the road in a RV during this time of the world going to hell in a hand basket because government did not want to scare anyone with impending doom news. I decided to try a new strategy, I approached John differently.

"You ever get a chance to do much trapping John?" I let him focus on while considering an appropriate way to bring up the next topic.

"Cant say that I have, Dave," he replied quicker than I expected.

"You think there's something to catch that way around here?" he said all ears and Sarah looked flummoxed.

"That's a beaver dam that looks like it's backing up that creek forming that huge pond." I replied looking off in the distance at the mouth of it.

"I thought that was just flotsam or jetsam." he said eying the odd contours of the pond's dams.

"I am going to sleep in one of these cars next to you, if I have permission to stay the night on your newfound land, and show you how to catch a beaver or a muskrat in the morning, if you would like." I said to John studying the lands features I had pointed out.

"What does a beaver taste like Dave? I hate to hurt the industrious creatures, but if it's not cruel, me and John might try one some day." Sarah said looking in the same direction as I and contemplating having a snare class in the morning.

"Well, they are smart as hell and taste like pork, kind of, but we don't have any lure so I got to think of an angle." I said still thinking of my next step.

"I think I heard in a pioneer day high school book report that the beavers tail the best eating." said John volunteered, regaining the conversation and a look of wonder from Sara.

"I've only eaten one twice during hard conditions, but the tail is fatty like a steak and you sizzle the hell out of it." I offered, dreading the chore of cleaning one in the field, if I got lucky.

"They got something called castor glands, to watch out for and collect, I think. I remember reading a Mountain man story of the fur trappers." Sarah suggested looking at me like I was the answer to not having to eat fish for dinner for the rest of her life.

"I haven't figured out why Beavers and cotton mouth snakes don't affect each other, but be careful around beaver dams. You are more likely to see a snake than a beaver and every animal uses the dams as a crossroads, easier to catch a coon than a beaver on a dam." I said drawing my audience in to the natural way of things.

"Folks eat rattlesnakes, supposed to taste like chicken." John said thinking about those brush piles for a moment."

"Tastes like chicken that's been eating fish." I said and let that sink in a minute. "I got 5 beers, and half of a half of gallon of whiskey, am I staying or what?" I tempted enthusiastically.

"We got CAMP RULES, David." Sara said awaiting John's reply as she continued eying me like a school teacher correcting one of her pupils.

"We can partake, but watch the cussing or confrontations." John said while reassuring his devoted one.

"I am sorry, Dave, old habits of old campgrounds, you've been an angel, you and the old man have a little fun." she said touching my leg and receiving a nod from her husband.

"It's been the start of hard times, and I haven't quite wrapped my head around it yet." said Sarah looking to John.

"'A toddy for the body does a soul good', sometimes" he said, hugging his wife of many years. ""You want one?" he questioned looking deep in her eyes as a touching moment transpired, revealing the depth of their devotion to each other.

"Sure, and I will play bartender, but you all play nice." she admonished. "And I might even have a little one with you, before I turn in for the night."

"We sharing the Coke Cola, John?" she queried

"Got to!" he responded as I rose to share libations with my new found friends.

20

TRAPPING SEASON

Hell, you could eat road kill and survive. I thought, as I remembered the reason for my heartburn and Sarah's cooking last night, upon waking in the air freshener imbued car I finally crashed in last night. Now it's 6am in the morning, gloom despair and misery on me. *They got any coffee they willing to share* I wondered, as I stretched the kinks of days journeying and the partying of last night out under the stars with John and his harmonica.

Oh hell, the morning after. I think me and Sarah danced a jig to Johns wailing music, if I remember rightly. Well, onwards and upwards, lemme think, oh yeah, John can weld and was going to attach a lawn service trailer to my rig today, if he was still willing. That's one art I never learned and we had talked about what good was that welding truck next to us with acetylene and oxygen tanks attached to the sides.

"Morning David, I will have us a cup of coffee going momentarily." he said fiddling with a camp stove.

"I sure am glad I got this Coleman multi fuel stove, especially seeing that gasoline isn't good for much these days."

"Be hard to run out of fuel for that out here, you won't have to hardly use your propane at all." I said watching him set the coffee pot upon it.

"Morning, David. We had us a real shindig last night didn't we." She said cheerily.

"That we did, John you still up for trying to weld a trailer hitch on my tractor after coffee?"

"Sure I will, it won't take long and would be my pleasure." he said arranging coffee cups on a small table.

"I might scc somc folks on thc road that need a ride to Montgomery on down this way and I got supplies to haul around once I get there." I said receiving a very welcome steaming mug of instant from Sarah.

"Having a trailer might be just the thing, if it doesn't slow me down too much." I offered.

"Sarah and I talked over your offer last night about taking us with you David, but we have decided to stay." he said settling down in his chair.

"We think we would be better off than most folk's right out here" he said knowingly and then carrying on. "It appears that we got water, food and shelter aplenty, so what more could we want? The cities are going to get real bad, David". He added.

"Yeah I am dreading city life during this mess, but I don't have any choice but to get there and bug in for now." I said wearily.

"John, that looks like some Sassafras trees over there on the bank". I said pointing

"The bark of the roots is used to make a pretty pleasant tasting "tea". The powdered leaves are used in Louisiana to thicken soup." I said while rising to go over to the bushes.

"Which ones? Show me." Sarah said excitedly and rose to join me.

"Sassafras is a tree with three different leaves. One is oval, one partly divided into three lobes, and one is mitten-shaped. The edges are smooth." I instructed when we got next to them.

"Here, smells this." I said as I removed a leaf and crumpled it and handed it to Sarah.

"Smells like Root Beer." she laughed.

"You can make tea with the leaves by pouring boiling water over a handful, letting them sit covered, away from the heat, 20 minutes, then straining out the leaves. But the roots of small saplings make an even better tea. You can use the root over again. To make root beer, chill the tea, then add drop of honey for sweetness. You can also chew on sassafras twigs to freshen your breath."

"Those mitten shaped leaves are easy to spot." Sarah said looking around. Why it's all over the place." she gushed, pleased with her backyard finds.

"People used to say it helps with rheumatism, but I just like the taste." I offered wandering back towards the RV

"Oh, I got an herbal book, I am going to go look it up." she said energetically reaching for the trailer's door.

"David, you have time to refresh me on snaring today, before you take off?" John inquired moving towards my tractor and surveying where the best place was to add a hitch.

"I can go over the basics while we are working on the tractor and we can put out a few sets, but then I need to get going." I replied, while following John over to the welding truck sitting on the side of the road.

I then began to explain about traps and snares, while John got together what he needed from off the truck.

"Snaring is one of the most efficient ways to harvest wild game and put meat in the pot. It takes less energy and a trapper will out produce a hunter any day. It is much easier to trap small prey than to hunt them. You'll have several empty traps for every success, but having several traps out means twenty four hours a day you're several times better off than a hunter.

When setting a snare, look for signs of fur around a tree's base or signs along a fence line to indicate where an animal has passed through. Animals will return to the same place to sleep and will continue to negotiate fences at the same spot.

Go hunting after you set traps, if you have a mind to, but I am sure your time and energy is better cherished doing other important tasks concerning other important current needs. To me sometimes-just rest is crucial."

John and I moved the tractor over to the welding truck and he was removing the hitch off the truck and getting ready to tack it on the back of the tractor as I continued.

"One tip I will tell you, John, is when you are walking animal trails, walk directly in the center of the trail. You don't want to be packing down the side of the trail and creating a new path or directing the animal away from your snare you have set dead in the middle of the trail." I said while admiring his handiwork.

"That ought to do her, let's go get the junk off that trailer." he said stepping away from his project.

"You know John, those lawn mowers probably got fried batteries, but I bet you could maybe get one running or with those welding skills of yours you could probably rig up those weed eaters to run you a cart." I said getting interested in the mechanical possibilities.

"Wow, great idea! I could cobble something together, I am sure given time and time seems to be what I got the most of nowadays." he said getting interested in the prospect of some transportation.

"I can see you and Sarah now, coming to visit on go-carts." I said laughing and pushing a lawnmower off the ramp.

"Dang, no keys, I wanted to try one just to see if maybe it would work." John said mournfully.

"You Boys want some more coffee?" Sarah called out.

"Sure, we need a break. "John answered and motioned for me to come on.

"Carry on teaching about snares and trapping, David." he said and so I did.

"I know this is survival situation, but save a bit of your catch as fresh bait for your traps when you can, if you're after meat eaters. Wear light cotton gloves to help keep your scent off the snares. Don't urinate etc. in the vicinity of your traps.

Stay busy and alert checking your trap lines in mornings and evenings. This productive activity will relax your mind and get you more attune with your environment and the animals you seek to ensnare. Let me give you a little clue here to help you, which most people never think about; Man is the only animal in the forest that just blunders about blindly going to his destination. Man walks continuously with very little pausing. Every other animal moves a bit, and then will stop to listen and look around and take in his environment, always looking for danger or listening to other animal's activity for signs of food.

Try it next time you are out in the woods. I don't mean just pause and a few seconds later go back to crashing about and dragging your feet through the undergrowth in a straight line. I mean really listen and sometimes get on down to animal level and look at things from their height. You will start seeing and hearing things much more acutely and become a much more natural predator yourself."

For the next hour or so I talked to John about snares and Sarah took notes for later use. John had some brass wire, as well as some picture hanging wire and we made up snares while we talked.

"Loop size and height should vary to match the targeted animal and also the conditions. Adjust the snare height to the approximate position of the animal's head If there is a lot of vegetation on the trail make snare a bit higher off the ground and most likely the animal will raise their head to slide their chin over the snare.

On some trails you can use sticks from the natural surroundings to narrow the trail a bit and direct the animal towards the center of the snare. You can also put a stick across the trail above the snare so that the animal will duck under it and into the center of the snare

Rabbits, muskrats, groundhogs, and other animals usually follow the same trails through meadows and forests and a good rule to follow is to make your trap's noose about 1.5 times the diameter of the head of the animal you wish to trap." I said and paused to jot down some particulars on Sara's notepad:

Coyote: 10-12" diameter loop, approx. 8-10" off of the ground.

Fox: 6-8" diameter loop, approx. 6-8" off of the ground

Bobcat: 8" diameter loop, approx. 8" off of the ground

Beaver: 9-10" diameter loop, approx. 2-3" off of the ground

Raccoon: 6-8" diameter loop, approx. 3-4" off of the ground

"John, you have experience hunting in the woods already, so I don't think it's necessary to have to go point out game trails to you. Sadly, I need to get on my way folks." I said wishing I didn't have to go.

John said rising "No, I got the jest of it, lets go hook up your trailer," he said.
"I wish you could've stayed longer." Sarah said, uncertain of what the future held and enjoying the company.
"I wish I could too, Sarah, but I have other responsibilities that need my attention." I said smiling at the old woman a bit wistfully.
We hitched up the trailer and after about 8 tries I got the old rattle trap tractor fired up and idling. I decided to reload my gear back on the tractor itself, in case I had to dump the trailer to get around some obstacle or in case of some emergency I hadn't anticipated yet, and turned to my highway castaways.
"Well, good luck John and happy hunting and fishing." I said extending my hand to him.

116

"I appreciate all the tips. Now, you be careful out there, you hear." he said gripping my hand and looking at me intently.

Sara spread her arms in a 'come to Momma' motion for a hug and said, "David, it's been a real nice visit. You have a good life and we will be thinking of you."

"I enjoyed it. Make John lots of Sassafras tea." I said smiling and looking to where she'd laid her herbal primer that she'd been studying and learning about all the medicinal properties of her new favorite potion in Nature's pantry.

"Oh, I will! I am going on a nature walk with my book later on today to find out what else grows around here." she replied happily and taking John's hand to hold.

"Well, good bye then, I'll be off now." I said mounting the tractor and putting it in gear. A final wave and I resumed the journey home.

21

On the Road Again

Just think in a few more hours, if this marvelous piece of junk holds up, and I will be home! I mused. Maneuvering around the stranded cars with the trailer was occasionally difficult, but mostly they were spread out enough to give easy passage.

There is a town or two like Tuskegee coming up that I'd just as soon not have to go through, even if the exits are few. I think its best to go the back way and although I would make better time on the interstate, I feel safer going the country route.

I had traveled some of these roads before and knew what to expect from summer vacation trips to Lake Martin. *Humm, how would that be for a possible bug out location, if I ever needed one?* I started contemplating. Half the time, people didn't use their lake houses and the year round residents were not many.

Fishing kind of sucked, because they constantly adjusted the lake levels according to power or water needs. *Well, the State wouldn't be tweaking on that for some time to come.* I said smiling to myself, but unsure if I needed to consider the possibility of flooding because of this.

There was plenty of game and water, lots of empty houses to scavenge, it sounded like a good idea. I guess it would really depend on the neighbors, because those lake places were built so damn close together, but with 750 miles of coastline, surely I could find something suitable.

I wonder if the lake house I rented off of my friends Jenny and Lyle would be empty. *Hell, they could be stuck there, but I doubted it. They lived a pretty good distance away from there and rarely went to the lake. It's not like I could call to find out.* I angrily thought, considering how the whole technologically oriented world was now all topsy-turvy.

Just then, a huge mutt came running down the driveway chasing my trailer and trying to bite at the tires.

My shouts of, "Go away and GIT" didn't faze it a bit, but it soon tired of the game at the end of 'his yard' and he trotted back. *Don't forget the dog problem, David, I reminded myself. It won't be long until strays and packs will be everywhere. It's a shame*, David considered, he really loved all animals but he needed to be thinking on how to protect himself and his loved ones from them.

I think when I get settled, I better minefield around my house with snares but that would have to wait until he saw the true condition of the city. I sure don't want to trap a neighbor's dog by mistake.

I started thinking about how I should've told John and Sarah about the possibility that dangerous feral dogs could threaten them in the future, when I saw a two car wreck up ahead blocking the road.

Damn, no getting around this, I thought, *nothing to do but get turned around and find another way.* If I remembered right, there was a road in back of me that headed in the Lake's direction, but I wasn't sure quite where it ended up.

Stupid map I had did not show all these little roads. Oh well, I guess I travel by dead reckoning for a while. If I get over lakeside, I can figure out where I am and cut back over, or maybe I could go check to see if Jenny and Lyle are up at their Lake cabin. The cabin's way out of my way, but that sounds like the best plan. Who knows, they might need a ride to Montgomery, although they still lived about sixty miles from it.

119

Would they want to go? If I were them, would I? They probably only had brought enough food with them for a few days and not much else, so the idea might be attractive to them. I bet Lyle at least had a 72 hour kit with him.

He was a Fireman and contingency planning sort of man in his blood, so they had at least that to help them get by. I wonder what he has in his. Certainly not the crap I normally lug with me when I go up there I thought thinking dreamily of my own setup at home that contained a Henry .22 survival rifle and an emergency snare kit. Hell, just having those two items would influence whether I stayed or went if given the chance to evacuate out of the same situation into the unknown or known dangers of the city.

I bet Jenny has her .357 with her though, but knowing Jenny probably only has six rounds for it, I was considering when I spied a couple walking down the road.

Humm, do they look safe? Hard to tell from here, but best to be careful. I thought adjusting my .380 pistol. I had it loaded with a nasty round called a Magsafe, which basically acted like a regular bullet as it penetrated and then opened up like a shotgun releasing pellets everywhere.

I thought about the company's literature on them. The now - famous Strasbourg Tests put MagSafe on the map. To Summarize what nearly everyone already knows, over 600 live French Alpine goats (their bodies are very much like humans) were shot under controlled conditions: no anesthetic, same shot placement form animal to animal, and with blood pressure and heart rate monitors to determine the Incapacitation Time (measure of how long it took a goat to cease functioning after the single shot was delivered).

MagSafe Ammo worked - better than anything else. However - and this is where things get interesting - there wasn't a jacketed hollowpoint bullet in ANY caliber which dropped the goats faster than MagSafe's weakest .380 load!

MagSafe's .380 beat every .45 ACP slug, every 10mm, every

9mm (including police-only ammo), every .40 caliber - no matter who made it - Cor-Bon, Remington, hydrashok etc.

So Basically, I had turned my puny .380 into a 45! I remember you are not supposed to put them in light frame guns like Kel-Tec but that Sig could take the heaviest loads of anything with no problem

"Hello Folks!" I said slowing down and applying the brakes.

"Hi, how did you get that thing to run?" asked a sunburned man his thirties carrying a small cooler.

"Long story. Where are y'all headed?" I said looking over at the profusely sweating heavy set woman with a garbage bag full of clothes.

"We got a cabin about 15 miles from here and we were heading there for vacation when this crap hit." she said looking anxious.

"I need to let this thing cool down." I said killing the engine "I might be able to take you there or at least get you a lot closer." I allowed.

"Oh, that would be a huge help. Thanks, my name is Randy and this is Sue," he said extending a sweaty palm in my direction.

"How far have you come?" I asked while motioning and telling them to put their meager possessions in the trailer.

"About thirty miles, I guess. I don't know, we been traveling down this road for days." Randy declared leaning up against the trailer.

"We just don't know what to do and some of the people living around here have just been so mean." she said looking at me imploringly.

Randy said "We have been run off from more than one house, when we asked for help. First couple days people seemed willing to help, but as time passed the mood seemed to change." he said dejectedly.

"And one of them had a GUN!" Sue interjected looking horrified.

"That guy scared the hell out of me." Randy said looking

back up the road to be sure nobody else was coming.

"How far back?" I asked becoming concerned.

"Oh, that was sometime yesterday." he said giving me instant relief.

"So you've been sleeping out in the open?" I asked grabbing a bottle of water off the tractor and offering it towards them, but Randy shook his head and produced one from his own cooler.

"No, we been sleeping in abandoned cars at night" she said looking worn out by the ordeal.

"Can you show me on this map where we are roughly." I asked.

"About right here." Randy said studying the map

"But that map doesn't show all the crossroads and lake drives that go to our cabin." he informed me while handing me back the map.

"Look, I will pay you if you can take us all the way." he said fumbling for his wallet.

"Not necessary, I will take you there. But you are going to have to really holler early if I need to turn. It's going to be hard to hear you back in that trailer." I said indicating where he and his missus would be riding.

"That tractor is pretty small." he said looking at the single bare metal seat I had.

"When we get closer, one of you can sit up front and give me directions." I said still considering the map.

"That will be fine." a greatly relived Randy said escorting Sue back and arranging them in my trailer.

"Takes me a minute." I told them as I went through the elaborate start up procedure for the tractor.

"You ready?" I hollered back over my shoulder and with a lurch off we went.

We got about 6 miles down the road with me missing most of the pot holes and not throwing them around too bad as I swerved back and forth changing lanes to avoid the occasional cars.

Randy shouted directions occasionally to me and I started

slowing as I approached a small gas station and looked it over slowly as I passed. The glass door of the front of it was busted in a one window was smashed and I speeded up and kept going down the road. Well, somebody has already looted that and I am not going to be the one accused of doing it this far out in the country where everyone probably knows each other. Randy hollered at me to pull over, so he could help navigate the twists and turns of the road back down to their lake cabin, as we crowded each other with him sort of perched on one fender, as his wife getting bounced all over the place in the trailer.

"It's the fifth drive on the left." he hollered over to me as we navigated the gravel road on the shore of the lake and I turned in.

"Home sweet, Home." said Randy cheerfully, as he climbed down off the tractor and then helped his wife up from the trailers bed.

"I am not complaining, Dave, but that was a hell of a ride!" she said looking even more of a mess than she did when she got on.

I laughed and said dryly she should, 'tell the county to fix the road' and we walked towards the cabin.

"We got some food in here, David, but we left most of our groceries behind in the car." Sue said forlornly.

"Yeah, stay for supper, Dave." said putting down the ice chest and opening a rancid freezer. "PHEW! We need to get this shit out of here right now!" He said grabbing a garbage bag and empting the foul smelling contents into a bag.

"Get it outside, but I got plans for that, so don't go chucking it in the lake or anything." I said watching Sue looking through the kitchen cabinets.

"What plans?" she said looking up at me speculatively.

"How many hooks you got? I want to build and run a trot line I said.

"Great Idea! But I don't think I got any line heavy enough to support it." Randy said.

"Oh, we will find something." I said eying the Venetian

blinds.

"Oh, no you don't, David." Sue protested seeing the direction my thoughts were taking.

"I was just thinking things through, your blinds are safe. I would say we could consider your neighbors, who don't appear to be at home, but I would give them several days to possibly arrive before messing with their stuff." I said peering out the window.

"Looks like we might have this point on the lake all to ourselves." she said joining me at the window.

"Well, that clothes line over there can stand to have one strand missing, if they do come home." I said looking inquisitively at her.

"Oh sure, get that, they shouldn't mind." she said and I went to get the nylon cord. As I was walking back, Randy called out, "Dave, how about a glass of wine?" while holding up an empty glass in one hand a bottle in the other.

Bleh I thought, I do not really like wine, hot wine at that, but it does contain alcohol.

"Yes, thanks." I said and joined him and Sue at the table.

"Want to try for a fish fry tonight?" I asked holding up the line. They looked hesitant, so I added. "I don't mean to impose on your hospitality, but I saw a hammock over there that would suit me for the night, if you want to try some night fishing?"

Looking relived not to have a stranger overnight in her house, Sue said that arrangement would be fine.

"Grab your tackle box, Randy, and I will start rigging a Trot line." I said while sipping the wine, while trying not to make a face.

"That stinking meat will be good for catfish, but I will put a few hooks a bit shallower in case it appeals to a bream or a bass, too." I said while measuring off monofilament line and tying it to the clothes line. "You can sink some of that meat in a can or something to attract fish while I make this thing Randy." I directed.

"I hate even getting around it, but ok, let me go find

something. He found a old paint can with some dried pant in it, added the meat and bent the lip over and tied a line to it and proceed past us with it held at arms length to the dock and threw it in. " Nasty stuff." he yelled up to us while washing his hands in the lake. Then he turned and came back to the table and reached for his wine.

"I'm going to tie this to the front of your boat and paddle it out a ways and anchor it. If you got enough rope I can use the cleat on the boat to make a retrievable clothes line like they use between building in New York, so nobody has to go swimming again to retrieve the fish." and then proceeded to outline my plan.

"So we just pull back and forth to bring the fish in huh, that's neat." said Sue grasping the concept.

We got the line baited and the rig set up and proceeded back to the table.

"Unless you got some light gauge wire, I need you to sacrifice one of your lamp cords." I said to Sue.

"What are you going to make now, Dave?" she said draining the last of the bottle of wine into our glasses.

"You might as well learn this trick too or you're going to get awfully tired of fish for supper." and began explaining about snares, as Randy returned with a lamp cord and a pair of wire strippers.

"If we catch some fish tonight after the line soaks for awhile, when we clean them we can use the guts for a bait pile and you can set snares for a Raccoon or a possum or something." I began before Sue interrupted me.

"But we got canned food, and I am not going to eat a possum!" she said adamantly.

"Well, suit yourself, that's the trick anyway, if you ever need it. I suggest though you don't wait to run out of food before you try it." I said pointedly.

"Well, I bet these houses around here have some food in them." she said looking about.

"Perhaps, you know about lake cabins, some people have

supplies and some don't even stock a can of beans. Be sure to boil your water and don't trust that lake." I said looking up at her.

"David, can you explain a bit more about that 'Carrington Event' thing again?" Randy asked and I proceeded for the umpteenth time to cover the basics I knew, as my audience huddled together. We checked the lines and got three good fish and Sue fried them up in cornmeal for us and we had dinner by kerosene lamp light.

Shots rang out from across the lake and somebody was yelling something, we could not make out and then it went quiet. It's amazing how sound travels across the lake at night and we couldn't make out where the noises had came from.

"You got anything for protection, Randy?" I got around to asking.

"I ain't got shit." he said miserably

"Then I would start breaking into houses tomorrow to see if you get lucky enough to find something and start carrying that fish knife you had out earlier." I suggested.

"You know how to use a gun?" I asked

"I shot a friend's once or twice, but no, not really." he replied.

I spent the next half hour or so telling him the basics of how different types of guns worked, in case he got lucky enough to find one. I also advised them to always try and stick together and not get to separated when they were doing fishing or scavenging.

"How did you estimate when Sundown was earlier, Dave?" Sue said cleaning up the dishes. "I haven't been able to figure how close that was for days after our watches stopped." she said while moving around with a flashlight.

"Well, for whatever reason mine's still working, but there is another way of doing it. How much time left before sundown? Hold out your hands in front of you at arms' length and, with the edge of a palm lined up at the horizon; see how many fingers you can fit between the horizon and the position of the Sun in the sky. Each finger width represents about 15 minutes." I said sitting back and watching the moonlight shimmer on the lake.

"I got to try that tomorrow." Randy said turning towards Sue. "We got anymore wine left?" he asked her.

"Well, one bottle but maybe we ought to save it?" She replied.

"To Hell with that, let's drink it now. Old Murphy's house has a full bar in it over there and I am paying that house a visit tomorrow." he said.

Well, ok." and she rose to go get it.

"Randy, a lot of these places have firewood stored around them, I would gather up all I could before winter, as a suggestion." I said offering my glass for a refill of the wine that suddenly didn't taste so bad to me.

"I better grab it before someone else does huh." he said watching the lake.

"Well, I am heading to bed soon, might as well tell you all good bye before morning, I will be setting out pretty early to go see if my friends are up here or not." I informed them.

"If they're not there, you're welcome back here, Dave." Sue said in her most neighborly voice.

"I appreciate it, but if they're not there, I will be heading for Montgomery next." I replied wondering what the tomorrow would bring.

"We will get up and see you off or maybe we can have breakfast and check the trotline in the morning?" Randy said hopefully and fidgeting with his wine glass.

"I will be waking up with the sun, if you hear the tractor fire up and want to make the effort of seeing me off, fine but after the trip you all had I suspect you will want to stay in bed awhile longer." I said contemplating a buggy night about to be spent in a hammock.

"You got any mosquito repellant?" I asked of Sue.

"Oh, come inside and be comfortable in your own bed, Dave. I am just not used to having strangers and you're a nice guy, so you're welcome to the spare room, if you like." she said good-naturedly.

"I will take you up on that, sounds much better than semi

roughing it, thanks." We sat around a bit longer and she showed me to my room. We said our good nights and I sank down into the soft bed without even taking my clothes off and fell fast asleep.

I saw the sun begin peeping in between the blinds, as I woke up bleary eyed and thirsty. I tip toed past the closed door of my hosts' bedroom and found a bottle of water in Randy's ice chest. I almost didn't take it; I felt I was committing the ultimate sin by doing so. Funny, how our concepts of value changes under circumstances like these. Hell, they got a whole lake and all day to boil water, it's not like I was leaving them without something, and I reassured myself and slipped out the door.

Ok, you old oil drinking machine, I said as I checked the dip stick and added my last two quarts of 40 weight oil. *Damn thing is probably going to get temperamental about starting now to. Hang on, I better check my gas. I am getting pretty low. I think one of these boats around here has what I want.* And I wandered over to the neighbor's. The boat had two cans full of gas, but no oil on board. They probably had some in that shed, but I didn't want to make a bunch of noise busting in, so I just carried the cans back and refilled the tractor. Randy came outside mid process and said good morning.

"You got any oil I can have?" I asked

"Yeah, I got a few quarts." he said turned to go get them, as I stowed the cans on the back of the trailer.

"Borrowed some gas, huh. You get that off my boat?" he asked uncaringly.

"No, I confiscated your neighbor's, you can tell them it was me if they show up, if you want." I said in my best smart ass manner and started going through the procedure of starting my steel mule.

" Ok, they can put out a APB on a guy on a tractor wearing suit pants and dress shoes," he guffawed and then added "I will tell them your name was Oliver Wendell Douglas." he said making aspersions to the lead in TV. series Green Acres.

"Good one." I said grinning and extending my hand. "Good

bye, Randy, tell Sue goodbye for me and thank her for the use of the bed." I said looking towards the house.

"She is out like a light, but I will tell her." he said shaking my hand.

"I guess we need to watch that expression now, Randy." I said looking bemused.

"Oh, yeah. Right." Randy said a bit worriedly.

"Stay safe." I said while warming up the tractor.

"I will try." he said waving as I put it in gear and began to rumble of with the trailer clattering behind me.

I glanced at his neighbor's houses as I chugged down the access road. Nobody to home, it looked like, but who could tell with cars and lights not being visible. Ah, I thought it's the houses with cars that are at home obviously, but empty driveways not necessarily and reminded myself to stay cautious.

I am considering losing this trailer; these narrow roads are making me think it's sort of impractical. Those look like wild turkeys on side of the road up ahead. Yes that's what they are; the birds started slowly moving to cover as I got closer.

You always see a lot of game on these roads coming up here. Me and my ex girlfriend Sherry counted 8 deer just in one weekend coming up here. I don't think they will be so tame, as soon as people start hunting them for food again, instead of just for recreation.

I hear a chainsaw off in the distance, see life goes on. This situation is really bad, but not as bad as most people will think it is. We are not totally back to the 1800s yet. A lot of stuff still works by design or lucky chance; it's just going to take a lot of getting used to.

Right now everyone is feeling the 'cascading effect' of an EMP event. If electrical power is knocked out and circuit boards fried, telecommunications are disrupted, energy deliveries are impeded, the financial system breaks down, and then food, water and gasoline become scarce. It is the being ready for this sort of thing and not panicking, that I have been preaching for years.

Even if people were not heeding the Sun's warning signs

NASA was monitoring, just taking an all hazards approach and preparing for something like a hurricane would help prepare them for something like this.

The government, all though it hasn't done a lot of EMP planning, has done some and has hardened a lot of its strategic and tactical communications systems. The phone company and the government have the emergency communication system beefed up to handle this, somewhat; but I remember from my studies, even though they have special concrete bunkers housing emergency communication equipment, they made sure to leave it unplugged just in case.

I am not sure exactly what we got hit with, if I can find an undamaged AM radio, maybe I can get some news. I know we have hardened transmitters for such, but who knows if the operators could get to work that day. That's the problem with planning for this sort of thing, too many what ifs and a government that doesn't like to think outside of the box.

.The private sector owns and operates a large majority of our critical infrastructures and key assets, but most haven't spent the money to prepare for anything like this, although the threat has been known for years.

I see my turn off ahead to get to Jenny's cabin and start slowing down for it. There are not too many houses on this point and several vacant lots still available that not too many people want, so it is a short drive down the access road.

I do not see any vehicles; they probably were not even close to here. I walk up to the door, knock, and holler hello. Nothing, just silence. I am considering going down to the lake to have a wash up before I carry on, when I hear, 'Hello!' and see a short old man walking towards the yard.

"Hi. I see Jenny and Lyle are not at home." I said careful to say I knew the couple, because cabin owners look out for each other, and also because he looked to be wearing an old Ruger hog leg pistol on his belt.

"Nope. Name's Bernie." he said relaxing and going into friendly lake neighbor mode.

"Mine's David. I was just coming by to check on them." I replied.

"I haven't seen anyone for over a week, except that neighbor across the slew over there." he said gesturing at the large brick house about 200 yards across the finger of the lake.

"Donnie is a retired weather man, he bicycled his way over here a day or so ago and explained to me what he thought had happened." Bernie said looking towards his house.

"I bet you didn't know anything happened for a day or two." I said knowingly.

"I thought the power was just out, but I did notice the lack of boat traffic on the lake and wondered what was up." Bernie said looking at my old tractor.

"You like my old heap, it's ugly and noisy as hell, but so far it's been a good ol' work horse." I said while moving towards some shade.

"I used to have one similar back on my Daddy's farm, they are pretty dependable." he replied and joined me in the shade.

"I see you might be expecting trouble." I said motioning towards his holstered weapon.

"I am not sure what's going on, I heard a lot of gunfire last night and I figured better safe than sorry. So I grabbed my old .357. I like this old single action, the sights are big enough for me to see." He said taking it out and replacing it rather quickly.

"I have a Blackhawk too, is that the 9mm/357 combo or just .357 model?" I asked looking down at the handle sticking out of the worn holster.

"It is just .357, I couldn't find one of the 357/9mm combo ones with extra cylinder when I was looking." he replied.

"I was about to start making me some lunch, would you care to join me?" Bernie said looking me over.

"I don't want to impose." I said not wanting to be offered more fish again and trying to possibly decline the offer.

"I got flapjacks and spam." he said as if it was the biggest delicacy in the world.

"Hey, sounds good, I appreciate it." I replied following him back towards his cabin.

"I got coffee, too." he chirped opening his screen door to his house.

"You just made my day!" I laughed and followed him into his kitchen.

He had a Camp Chef outdoor camp oven perched on his regular electric stove and had it hooked to a big tank of propane instead of a canister.

"I always wanted one of those." I said admiring it.

"She works great." he said taking an old granite ware coffee percolator off the top and getting an extra cup out of his cupboard for me.

"Real coffee?" I exclaimed in anticipation and looking big eyed.

"I don't like instant, if you want sugar or canned creamer I got that." looking at me questionably.

"Black is fine." I said receiving my mug and relishing its aroma as he sat down with me at the kitchen table.

"You going to stay at Jenny's awhile?" he said taking a sip out of his cup.

"No, I am headed to Montgomery, but I think I will drop that trailer over there." I said looking across the table.

"I heard that thing rattling all the way down the drive. Might be a good idea if you trying to travel faster or quieter." he remarked looking out on the lake.

We talked about my trip in from Atlanta and what conditions of the roads were in, while he puttered around the kitchen putting together a meal for us. I asked him which roads he suggested, because I did not really want to have to drive all the way through the middle of the small town Tallassee to get back on the interstate, in case someone decided they wanted to take my trusty old ride.

"Well, you can go back down the way you came in and just head due south, when you get a chance." Bernie offered in between bites of one of the best meals I'd had in a while.

"I always get turned around up here. Which way is South from here that skirts the towns?" I complained.

"If you got a watch, I'll teach you a neat trick." he said nodding in affirmation and carrying on after I held mine up.

"It's called orienting by watch: Hold the watch level, point the hour hand at the sun. South is midway between the hour hand and #12 in the smallest angle." He said demonstrating

"That's a useful thing to know thanks." I said trying it out for myself.

"Hey, David, you could do me a favor since you're headed that way. I got a friend I want you tell I am 'doing ok' if you would." While watching me, but already reassured I would stop on my way.

"His name is Roland Stiles. He has a horse farm about 10 miles from the interstate and he will show his appreciation for you stopping to tell him I'm okay." he said, meaning there could be a reward in doing it for him.

"He doesn't happen to have kin in Newnan named Philburn Stiles does he?" I inquired.

"He sure does, you know Philburn?" he asked excitedly and gazed at me intently.

"I just met him about three days ago." I laughed and carried on. "Boy, do I have a story for you!" I replied draining my cup and starting to gather up the dishes.

"Those dishes can wait; I want to hear about how you come to know that old skin flint uncle of Roland's. Lets go down to the dock, where it's cooler." he said and pushed his chair back and lead the way.

"Well, he is not so tight fisted anymore." I replied and commenced to tell him how I acquired the tractor and how Philburn had to ride home on the back of an ugly purple girls bicycle.

"Ha! Ha! HA! That is the funniest shit I have heard in a long time. I need a beer after that. You want one?" He said pulling a burlap bag up by a rope that was soaking in the water at the edge of his pier. "I can't wait to hear about the look on Roland's face when you tell him that story." Bernie said chuckling and handing me a beer

"So that's my tractor story." I declared and popped the top on a semi cool can of refreshment.

"I don't know Ray, but if I ever get to see him, I sure want to shake his hand for getting one over on ol Papa Stiles." Bernie said still sniggering and looking towards the tractor we had been discussing.

"What do you want me to tell Roland when I see him?" I asked, turning back towards Bernie and enjoying the lake view once more.

"Tell him, if he can, to check on me come Christmas, I would be obliged, if he don't get by before then. Come to think of it, tell him late fall might be good, I don't have any wood cut for winter and I will probably be burning whatever I can get in order to get by." he said reconsidering and growing silent.

"I saw a house around the bend with about half a cord stacked up. If no one's to home I will transfer it here, if you want." I offered, wanting to repay his kindness of food and libations.

"Which one, that old blue house with the green looking shutters you say? Those folks live in Birmingham; they hardly ever make it down. I would dang sure be obliged if you would David. I won't be much help cause of my high blood pressure, but I will help you to get it." He said looking very grateful.

"You just enjoy the hay ride up and back. If anyone is around to object, I want a local to explain what it is we're doing and I would like the presence of that old hog leg of yours around, too, if I run into any trouble." I said while sucking the bottom out of the can.

"I will go you one better than that, I will get my 20gauge and ride shotgun," he said laughing and going for another pull on the rope to get us each another beer.

"David, I got a proposition for you." he said looking at me determinably

"I am listening." I said.

"Let's go get that weatherman over there to help." he said rising and waving at the neighbor on the opposite side of the slue, who had just appeared and was looking in our direction. "Hey!" He yelled over to the man, while waving his hands and gesturing for him to come to the edge of the water, so they could hear each other.

"I need your help moving some firewood, can you help?" he called back across the water.

"I can ride my bike over later." the man reluctantly called back.

"We got a tractor that runs!" Bernie yelled gleefully back.

"Do what?" the perplexed man called back.

"Hang on a minute." Bernie yelled, then to me, "David, can you fire that thing up and pull it around the house so he can see?" Bernie asked me while yelling out again, "Just a minute!" to his near, but far neighbor.

"That thing's cantankerous, but I will get it going." I said hurrying towards it.

"Just sit tight over there. I got something to show you." Bernie hollered back across water as the other guy made a motion towards his gazebo and headed that way to take a seat and wait for the unknown surprise.

Bernie headed over my way to watch me sweating over cranking the old beast. He was pretty good about not offering too much advice and when it fired up he hopped on the fender beside me, just like he had done the same thing a hundred times before, and pointed towards the backyard of Jenny's cabin. As we rounded the house I could see the man had already heard the thing and had jumped up and was beckoning for us to come on over looking like an overzealous sports fan.

"Be there soon!" Bernie tried to holler back to no avail and just waved the guy back to his house.

"Let me get my shotgun and grab the rest of the beer and we can go over there." he said dismounting.

Bernie came back and climbed up in the trailer and situated himself, while I put the beer in an empty tool box welded to the frame on the side of the engine.

"All set." Bernie hollered and I liked to have took the poor guy of his feet, as I released the clutch and brake and headed up the drive way.

"Sorry!" I yelled to non-hearing ears behind me and gunned it up the hill causing him to lurch again.

I thought I heard, 'slow down', and adjusted the throttle to a more moderate speed and looked back at Bernie holding on for dear life with his shotgun constantly falling off his small framed shoulder as we hit ruts in the road.

'You can't drive worth a shit!' I think he was mouthing at me, as I slowed and pointed to a turn up ahead to the right, just nodding his head and too fearful to let go of the trailers side rails to make a hand gesture, but looking like he was having a ball. Every time I would have to hit a pothole, that trailer with no weight on it would jump in the air and the little 95 lb man would go airborne a few inches, no matter what speed I was going.

We turned in front of the weatherman's house with a cloud of dust, even though I was going slowly, the trailer rose up one wheel as the other side lurched over a pothole, and the whole frame of the cheap trailer did a flexing jig to accommodate it. I was doing the shut down process on my rig and Bernie had already hopped out of the trailer and gave me a nasty look as he went to greet his friend, who had barely had a chance to vacate an expensive looking cast iron ornate plantation chair.

Donnie looked quite interested, but very confused about the circus sideshow that had just arrived in his front yard and turned speechlessly to his attractive, but equally dumbfounded wife who was exiting out the front door searching for the source of the racket she'd heard from inside.

I finally killed the engine to an instantaneous silence and was looking over at the group standing on the front porch with Bernie grinning, and Donnie's wife motioning at my hair, to remove some leaves and debris I had picked up on the way exiting the narrow driveway at Jenny's place.

"This is David." said Bernie trying to straighten his appearance and move his bangs back over his sweating bald spot and gesturing for me to come on.

" How come that things still running." she said taking in my dirty blue T-shirt cut off sleeved looking affair with dress pants and worn out dress shoes. "You said nothing runs." accursedly at her husband who was regaining his composure.

"I didn't think anything would." he stammered as Bernie encouraged him forward with a hand on his back to shake my hand.

"David Dupree." I stated presenting a grimy and sweaty palm.

"I am Donnie and this is Lisa." he said pointing at her and flinching, as I squeezed his hand in an honorable firm hand shake, noting how he started wiping his own on his shorts afterwards unconsciously. I didn't even try to shake his wife's hand, who was looking horrified at the prospect of taking this stinky wretch's hand.

"Look, I made prospect to Dave to help us get wood in for the winter, if you would help us." said Bernie latching a hold of the yuppies arm and turning him around.

"He is going to allow us to haul some wood on his trailer, if you and Lisa help." he said pointedly and reattached his grasp to a totally confused Lisa and led her back towards the shade of the porch and the wrought iron bench beside the chairs.

"Now hear me out." he said sitting the debutante down on the bench and taking a place next to her while Donnie and I took up individual chairs. "If David agrees to my deal, we can raid a couple of vacant houses for already chopped and seasoned firewood and be ready for winter!" he said looking around his audience for agreement.

"It's the middle of July!" the couple started to object, before the realization of their plight started to sink in and Bernie was allowed to continue uninterrupted.

"I got 5 silver dollars and a BUCK Knife, for three hours worth of work, David. And I know which homes to hit, because Roland's pulp wood crews service most folks around here and been buying firewood off him for years." he said in my direction quite satisfied with his plan, but waiting for my counter negotiation.

"How much wood do you figure we can collect in three hours?" I said remembering he had lessons from the horse trading Stiles clan and not appreciating what kind of efforts my dubious helpers were willing to produce.

"Oh, I don't know, maybe a few cords." he countered looking obviously expectant. I started to tell him he was crazy to expect that much work out of this crew, before Lisa started babbling about stealing. Not doing that kind of work, and just wait for FEMA to fix her life etc. before Donnie said they needed a private conference and went back inside the house to confer.

"I made you a fair offer David." an unpleased Bernie advised heading towards the tractor to grab the beer and leaving me to consider just what the hell I was getting into.

" I can go six pieces of silver, the Buck knife, and if I got any ammo for it, that gun you got hid about as well as the hooters in a wet T shirt contest." he said causing me to reflect and look at my waistline.

"It ain't the money buddy." I started to say, but then Lisa and Donnie came out the front door again looking resigned and not happy with me or my presence.

"I am willing to help, but I got to get going soon. We grab what we can in a couple hours and I'll just accept the Buck knife." I countered to Bernie.

"Well, I guess it's not fair to keep you, seeing as how you got your own family to go look out for." Bernie said resignedly.

"I suggest we start at the furthest house and work our way back." I said standing up and getting ready to try to push the crew to quicker activity and headed for the tractor.

Except for having to drive very slowly so nobody fell off the stacked wood, the trip was uneventful. Bernie had a general idea of who would not be on the lake this time of year, and the few people we saw just look surprised or scared at our appearance of hauling wood amidst this hot summer day and chaos.

Bernie looked at me for a moment and said "David, you think you will get back up this way? You said something about maybe bugging out to the lake if it got too bad in Montgomery."

"I am thinking it's highly possible, would you mind me taking over Jenny's place, if they are not here when I get back? I said while resurveying the place.

"You are always welcome Dave; there are plenty of empty houses around, if they do show up. I know I would like for you to come back, David." he said hoping for the best.

"I might see you come the fall, possibly." and I left it at that, while wondering if it might not be sooner.

We got the wood thrown off at both houses, with a portion at Jenny's, for good measure and said our farewells, as I refueled and oiled up before putting the tractor in the wind towards Montgomery with what I hoped was only to be a brief stop off at Bernie's friend Roland's house.

22

Homeward Bound

I reconsidered dumping the trailer after finding it so useful to help Bernie out and I had my own junk I needed to figure out how to haul around when I got to Montgomery. I had most of my long-term preps in storage because of my planned move to Atlanta and I had not yet devised a plan to move them over to my Moms house once I got home.

Moving my supplies out of that storage building is going to really take some planning on my part I realized. First off, it was in a neighborhood where I did not want a lot of attention drawn to me getting boxes out of the storage shed after an event like this, because it would be obvious that my unit contained food and secondly the gate in front of it was electric.

I had planned on that gate being down from a power outage earlier and had bought some bolt cutters to go through the fence if I ever had too, but they were in my truck stuck in Atlanta. I needed to know what the conditions were in Montgomery before I pondered a plan further though, just too many "what ifs" to deal with for now.

I found the back road Bernie had directed me too and the houses were few and far between on this deserted wooded stretch heading towards the interstate. There was very little traffic stranded on it and I made good time heading for Roland's place.

I slowed as I started seeing the white wood pasture fence leading up to the front gate and turned in. Damn, gate is tightly padlocked, figures I thought. I forgot to ask Bernie if Roland had any kind of dog, that was not good thinking on my part, I should have known better than to overlook that detail.

Well that house is pretty far away but I think I will try hollering at it before jumping a stranger's fence and wondering up. "HEY, ROLAND! ROLAND STILES! I called while watching the house and the barn. I tried again ROLAND STILES! I yelled.

A tall man in a cowboy hat exited the Barn and peered in my direction. "Who is it? He called back

"Message from Bernie" I hollered back to him becoming tired of this yodeling contest already.

"Just a minute, I am coming" he yelled back, went back in the barn, and led out a beautiful paint horse, which mounted and rode in my direction. I noticed he was carrying a lever action rifle too. He looked like vision out of the old west as he trotted up to the gate.

"Who are you and what's this message from Bernie?" he asked, taking in the old tractor and my odd dress.

"My name's David, I've just come from the Lake and Bernie said to stop and give you a message on my way to Montgomery." I replied looking up at the gaunt cowboy.

"You going to Montgomery on that thing?" he inquired while dismounting his horse and digging in his pocket for the key to the gate.

"Going to try to, I came from Atlanta on it so far." I said laughing.

"Well, pull it in and come up to the house." I will lock the gate up behind you.

I drove up the driveway to the red brick farmhouse and shut down the engine. He told me as he passed he was putting up the horse and would be back in a few minutes and to have seat on the porch.

He walked over to me, beamed a smile, and extended his hand "Name's Roland. Is Bernie alright? He is not hurt is he?" he said looking at me directly, but not overly concerned.

"He's doing fine, just out of power like the rest of us." I offered.

"I thought I was losing my mind when that storm hit. I was out bush hogging and my tractor died. Then, when I come back to the house, the power was out. The next morning my truck wouldn't start and I sort of put two and two together, but I thought it was nuclear until I heard about it on the radio." he advised me.

"You got a working radio? So what did they say?!" I anxiously began with a thousand other questions running through my head and on the tip of my tongue.

"Well, reception is spotty as hell, but a solar storm took out the grid and the president is saying it will take months for some areas and years for others to get power back." Roland replied nodding his head as if to say yea it is that bad.

"Not that I expect anything out of them, but did the reports say anything about FEMA trying to mount a response?" I was curious to know.

"They say FEMA is mobilizing, but it will take most cities a month or more to receive assistance." Roland said dubiously.

"Ah, they are bull shitting the public to keep them calm." I said agreeing to Roland's unsaid assessment.

"I figured as much, too." Roland said rising and telling me to come inside that I must be thirsty.

"FEMA doesn't even have a plan for something this big, and their personnel will be spread all over the place with hardly anyway to contact them." I said accepting a cool glass of water

Roland had poured from a stoneware crock sitting on the kitchen counter.

"I ain't expecting anything out of them, but I sure feel sorry for the folks in the cities as the grocery shelves empty." he said doing his wise nod.

"Hell, most of our National Guard is stuck somewhere in the Middle East. I do not know how they going to keep any kind of order as things unravel." I said as he refilled my water glass.

"So, what message do you have from Bernie?" he asked settling back in his chair.

I told him Bernie's message and worries about getting by in the cold winter and what little I did for him, while I was there to help get him ready for it.

"That was awful nice of you, David. Bernie is a good friend of mine. You want to stay over the night and have supper with me?" he inquired leaning back in his chair and clasping his hands behind his head.

"No, I need to be moving on soon, but Bernie said we should share a few beers and let me tell you a story about Philburn." I told him in anticipation of a little fun rest break before I got back out on the road.

"You know Philburn?" he queried, becoming all attentive.

"I sure do, that used to be one of his tractors sitting out there." I said with some mirth.

"Oh, I gotta hear this, let's go out to the barn for the beer." he said rising.

"I got a surprise for you, David, this beer is ice cold." he said turning and proudly grinning at me.

"How did you manage that?" I replied full of interest.

"I had me some marine batteries stored in the barn that weren't hooked up when this shit hit the fan and I got them hooked up to an inverter and a small portable ice maker." He said anxious to show off his setup. He had a solar panel charging his batteries, so that must of not got damaged either, but he said he was careful to unhook it in case the sun wasn't done with us yet.

"Ah, a really cold beer." I told him after taking a swig and proceeded to tell him my tractor story and Philburn's ride home on the back of Martha's bike.

Roland was laughing about Philburn getting the worst end of a deal and in particular about the bike.

"I know that damned bike. Martha, when she was a young girl, used to ride it in the town's parades and Philburn always commented on how god awful ugly it was." whooping with the hilarity of it all. "I would sure have paid good money to see you and him heading down the road on it! Ha! David and you say he got stuck with that thing in trade, too?! That is even better." he replied handing me another beer.

"Well, I could sit around and do this all day Roland, but I need to get moving soon." I told him as I looked out at the road.

"Well, I will give you a six pack to take with you, it won't get hot by the time you finish it. I seen you drink." he said kidding me good-naturedly and putting it in a plastic garbage bag.

"That sounds like fun." I said as I envisioned rolling along and catching a buzz on the way home.

"Let me see that pea shooter you got in your waistband." he said wanting to inspect my pistol which I then handed him.

"Sig 230, nice weapon, but a bit small of a caliber for my tastes. I got an extra .45 if you want to trade?" he said handing it back.

"No, I will keep it. I like it and I am having a hard enough time concealing it, let alone a 45." I replied finishing my beer.

"Well, at least I can give you a better shirt, unless you going to do that Larry the cable guy thing and cut the sleeves off." he said looking at me impishly.

"I won't customize it." I laughingly assured him and waited for him to come back with a shirt and started getting the tractor cranked up.

"I will ride up on the tractor with you and unlock the gate then walk back." he said handing me a short sleeve blue denim shirt, which I swapped for my sweat soaked threadbare T-shirt.

Roland opened up the gate and waved me off as I saluted him

with a beer and a smile as I headed on back down the road.

I checked my watch and it said 3.30. It is about 10 miles to the interstate and let us see about 30 minutes by car to the first Montgomery exit which be would be about 2 to 2 ½ hours on this thing, so maybe I get to my first stop around 6.30, if I was lucky.

I started reviewing my options and wondering if it was better to try coming in at night or daylight and which was the best route to take to my destinations.

I certainly don't want to risk the bypass exit. There are hotels on both sides of it and I bet they are going to be filled with stranded people and possibly a police presence. Montgomery has a bunch of cops and I would not put it past them to organize a receiving station or something.

Humm, if I was a cop in Montgomery and I broke down on the bypass, what would I do? I pondered while dodging disabled vehicles and feeling a bit lightheaded. Most of them would know what EMP was and many would just head for home to protect their families or a few might try for the supermarkets expecting trouble, but wanting supplies.

They got a bunch of bicycle cops in the city and some kind of response might have been organized by now, but what could they really do? I do not want my tractor commandeered by some cop that thinks he needs it more than me, so I guess I had better go in the back way to be safe.

Then, which direction should I go; I was thinking and mentally mapping out bad neighborhoods or possible traffic choke points etc. as I headed further down the road.

I see up ahead a few small groups of people heading towards Montgomery who are looking back at me evidently hearing me approach. I guess I am going to play shuttle service to town now, if they want to come in from the east instead of the center.

I slowed the tractor and asked a group of 5 people if they wanted to go to Eastdale Mall and they all enthusiastically agreed and climbed onto my trailer. I picked up 3 more a little further down the road and everyone looked bone weary and dirty. I wonder how many of these people knew each other or were together before they broke down in mass and left on the road. These particular folks must have been around 50 miles out to be still wandering in to town.

I made my turn and proceeded a few more miles before one of them hollered for me to stop, and with wave they continued on, grateful for the few miles I had saved them. I looked ahead on the road and there was no way I was going to make it much further pulling this trailer.

Traffic and wrecks were littering the road and as far as I could see were disabled cars and trucks that wouldn't be moved for a long time to come. I zipped around some parking lots and got everybody as close as I could before dropping the trailer and making a convoluted path around traffic by riding medians and ditches and even had to turn around once or twice.

I finally shortcut through a neighborhood and even went through somebody's backyard to get back on the road that would lead me to my first stop.

I was going to see Sherry and although we did not date anymore, we were very close friends. During the four years we dated, as well as afterwards, we had amassed preparations for almost every contingency and had a pact with each other to get through times like these.

I sure hope she was safe and had been close to home when the EMP hit. She always had her 72-hour kit in her car, so unless she had gone out of town for some unforeseen reason, she should be fine. One of her sisters lived close by to her, so I bet she was with her at the house. I am glad we were able to prep some for her also over the years, as Sandra didn't believe in putting back much more than you would in getting ready for hurricane season.

Damn, that food store must have caught hell. I thought as I looked at overturned buggies littering the parking lot and a busted front glass door. *I guess the shit has already started in some places here.* As I was traveling, I saw many what I supposed were neighbors out talking to each other in the streets.

I knew all about how disasters will bring people together for the common good short term, but I had little academic knowledge about how they were going to act long term with the necessities of life getting in shorter supply daily.

I could only imagine how those neighbors would be acting in the coming weeks. Most people live paycheck to paycheck and rarely even have two weeks worth of food in the house and maybe a few days worth of water if they had any at all. Water, geez, I wonder if the water would be still on. Natural Gas, I know would probably stay on for a while; I had no idea if the water company had any contingencies except for generators that may or may not be hardened.

There are no governmental rules to force them to do anything and if the company had not made an investment, we were in deep doodoo. There are no mandatory procedures or required emergency actions that require them to do anything, although they have known the threats for years.

NASA's "Solar Shield" satellite-based detection system at the Goddard Space Flight Center monitors coronal mass ejections. The U.S. grid currently relies for its defense on warnings from NASA that would alert U.S. utilities to take actions to protect their systems, but they would only have a few hours advance notice.

The stockpile of spare transformers would fall far short of replacement needs. Urban centers across the continent would be without power for many months or even years, until new transformers could be manufactured and delivered from Asia. The transformers are not made in the United States so there's no telling if or when we might possibly get a shipment.

I just do not know at this point, until I start sifting through some news, how bad off we are. I considered as I abruptly swerved to avoid some people that did not have sense enough to not stand in the road. *Damn people, though, are going to be their own worst enemies and I bet we already have catastrophic casualties.*

The hospitals probably filled the morgues over night, as back up generators started running out of fuel, unless someone had the initiative and the equipment to siphon diesel out of some trucks.

I had better watch my ass out here as most people by now have figured out they could pretty much do what they want without worry about the law. I had better be sure to let Sherry know it's me beating on the door or I might be looking at a 12 gauge or 9mm carbine, as a welcome home.

That neighborhood she is in is a strange one; you got professionals up and down the block and a few streets over various kinds of riff raff. On Fourth of July or New Year's, it sounds like a war zone with fools shooting off all sorts of weapons, I can only hope they are short on ammo about now.

I think when I get over to Sherry's house; I will hide the tractor in the garage and borrow her bike to go check on my Mother.

My Mom, she has to be freaking by now. She will be worried about me in Atlanta, as well as my brother in Texas. Not so much Bob, she knows he has been prepping for years the same as me and he is the one with his bigger salary that stockpiled some of her house. She wouldn't allow the level of stuff we wanted in the house, didn't see the need, but she did get on the bandwagon enough to bring in about a month and a half worth of supplies and various survival tools.

I got a bunch of stuff stashed in my closet and the majority of my guns there. I have sufficient ammo too, but not all. I got to thinking once again of my treasure trove of preps over at my storage building.

I got a good assortment of essentials over at Sherry's, I started thinking. Thank the Lord, she allowed me to stage some supplies over there that my dear old Mom would not allow me to, not seeing the expense or need, as well as her tenacious need for everything to be picture perfect in a room.

I do not have any pressing need to get to my storage building and I considered just leave it as it sits. The laws of natural selection will be taking over soon and in a month or two I will have less or greatly weakened folks to deal with.

On the other hand, though, if the State does organize some sort of response, it is going to be hard to get to with any kind of curfew in place. Damn, David I said fussing at myself, if anyone should know what they are going to do, you should, but all your degrees and licenses don't mean shit when you know they going to fly by the seat of their pants, even if they do manage to make an effort and organize something. Martial law will be a given, because of the stupid Patriot Act, but who will enforce it? No, it is going to be dog eat dog for awhile until humanity emerges again and civilization reforms itself just like it always historically does. What that will be only time will tell I guess.

No sense dwelling on it I guess until you get your facts I mused. The main thing is water, is it on or off. I was halfway tempted to pull the tractor over and try somebody's faucet on the side of their house the question was nagging at me so much.

I had less than 15 gallons at my Mom's. Sherry was ok, her neighbor Helga next door had a pool and between filtration devices and all the knowledge, she accumulated off me for years there was no problem there, except for our garden in her backyard and these series of droughts we had over the years were going to be taking a toll on my efforts to permaculture.

Sherry's backyard garden with 20 raised beds was a valuable commodity now and I had heirloom seeds in sealed cans to keep it going for some time to come. That was a funny thing about us, we always bought stuff in twos knowing that someday my job would take me away from her and we would separate as equals on the preps.

I supplied the larger portion of our food and safety insurance by using my school refund checks from studying emergency management and she allowed me to do this by paying for her house and helping me when I got low on daily living expenses. Looking back on all the arguments, we had on this odd couple arrangement we were both more than satisfied by the final outcome with a safety net or savings account we could have never produced alone.

The majority of the food had 25-30 yr shelf life and we were in our fifties so what would a can of Mountain House be worth in 20yrs if we needed it? Double, triple, quadruple the prices we paid? I already have seen the price of the stuff go up 35% since we started collecting it.

NASA said 2012 to 2014 for the Solar Storm to hit; various others prophesy for thousands of years said 2012 watch out. I saw economic collapse as a possibility or pandemic as not a possibility but a probability of happening and we decided to be as prepared as we could through part hobby, part necessity.

That reminds me, Sherry's old somewhat anti prepper friend Betsy will be finding her way to Sherry. There was no way in the world to hide our ever-mounting pile of goods and survival equipment from her, but it eventually just became a David and Sherry thing that was no longer talked about like a friend that had eccentric hobbies.

Well, I knew this day would come, I sighed to myself. Sherry and I were going to stop our constant monthly expenditures after the shear bulk of supplies reached a year apiece, but our Prepper hearts knew we must share and therefore just kept adding on in order to be not caught short when sharing with those that had not taken our path towards preparedness.

Now this day was upon us and we had what we had to ameliorate some misery with no re-supply in sight. I remember how many times I thought, probably wrongfully on the credit card scale, do I need anything else, will my shipment get in on time, etc.

Well, if I do not have what I need now, chances are I cannot find it again. I resolutely assured myself that I had taken prior proper actions.

23

The Arrival

Ok, final turn coming up, not a whole lot I can do about my appearance, but I start fiddling with my hair and trying to get the sweat off my face anyway before I turn in her driveway and zip around her car to get it ready to go in the garage. I smell wood smoke I am thinking, as my favorite cat dog appears to great me. Sally Cat always runs to say 'hi' to me and sounds like she is saying 'Davie! Davie!' In her meow meow voice.

We call her a cat dog because she has dog like tendencies and follows me around like a pup if I am in the area.

"Hello, Sally Cat, where is mamma?" I say as the back gate opens and Sherry and I rush to great each other.

"David, you're safe!" Sherry says hugging me and flinching at my whiskered face, as I nuzzle her back.

"Hey, Betsy. Sandra." I say over Sherry's back at the two faces appearing around the entrance to the gate and looking startled at my odd entrance on a tractor, but nonetheless looking pleased.

"Hi." the two in chorus and stepped out, as I put my arm around Sherry and escort her back towards them.

"What's for dinner and who has a beer?" I said to an immediate response of laughter and giggles

"Where did you get the tractor, Dave?" Betsy said sort of beyond herself with my strange arrival.

"That is a story unto its own, I take it we lack alcohol?" I said to my familiar tribe of friendly faces.

"Not a drop, we went through it almost day one." Sherry said dejectedly.

"I got a half gallon of George Dickel that a man named Donnie donated to the cause in that tool box on the side of the tractor..." I barely got out before volunteers a plenty started to go retrieve it and Helga came out of her house to see what the commotion was all about.

"David, welcome home! She boisterously said.

"Good to see you! You want to join us?" I offered following Sherry and a bottle I did not want to lose sight of.

"Maybe later." she called back and returned to her own home.

"We got water?" I said immediately reaching for the tap once inside the kitchen.

"Don't try to drink that!" came the admonishments from the girls and horrified looks from all around.

"We got boil water warnings David," Sherry said heading towards a 5-gallon bottle and a Harbor Freight pump set up.

"We heard it on the radio but there is an Army truck that comes by broadcasting it to" Sandra pointed out.

"That little crank EPSON is receiving then?" I directed my question towards Sherry

"See, darling, I do listen, it was in the steel file cabinet and works fine." she said looking pleased with herself.

"I noticed the guns, you just prepared or having problems," I said inquiringly.

"Well, you occasionally hear someone shooting one off, but I locked and loaded every one in the house as soon as I managed to get home, just like you said to do if this ever happened David." Sherry said confident of her leadership role.

"Were you at work when it happened?" I asked Sherry

"No, Betsy and I were working on our side entrepreneurial business and got caught totally unaware." she began before Betsy interjected her comments.

"Sherry made me lug that 2 quart canteen FULL of water all the way over here, even after I showed her the taps still worked." She pouted

"I already told you why you had to." Sherry began before Betsy cut her off.

"But, I had my clothes bag with me, too, and that canteen is heavy." She said indignantly.

"Coffins are heavier." I began but let the subject drop picking up a clue to do so from Sandra.

"This stove thingy you bought Sherry works real good." She said motioning towards a Stove Tec rocket stove.

"Does that water pasteurizer kettle thing work good, too? Sherry got me one off the same web site also, that funnel shaped water jacket inside of it is supposed to make it very efficient." I responded looking at what looked like a giant stainless steel two-gallon teakettle.

"I can't imagine being without it, it seems to be heating water for something all day." she said in her best 'told you so' voice.

"I can certainly see its uses." I conceded and thought how nice it was to be back amongst this happily bickering trio.

"David, I biked over to see your Mom yesterday and she is doing fine. " Sherry told me while placing a hand on my leg briefly and looking at me compassionately.

"Hey, I really appreciate you doing that, it means a lot to me." I said thankfully and reached for the drink Betsy was handing me.

"I am really glad you spent the extra money and got the wood/charcoal model of that stove, Dave. We cook the big meal using charcoal and use the extra burn time to heat water to wash the dishes in sometimes, but I want to save as much charcoal as we can, and besides with the right wood in it, it makes its own charcoal." Sherry said gesturing at the various piles of sticks and twigs everyone had collected.

"You all have been busy." I said admiringly looking at all the efforts that had taken place in the privacy-fenced back yard.

"She has been ordering us around to do some project or another every day. This morning's project was to take those green tarp like sheets out of those British personal protection units you bought a pile of and cover the windows so our lanterns don't shine out as a beacon to the street thugs." looking suspiciously on a self approving Sherry. "David, did you really buy sandbags, too? What the hell for?" she said looking at me.

"They go under the windows of this wood frame house if there is a need, but I will talk on that later. Right now I want more news and another drink, does anyone else want one?" I asked while heading towards the backdoor.

Various "I am ok" responses come back and I peeked into the living room to see the latest transformations. Not a whole lot had changed; it was in typical hurricane party configuration with extra bedding for guests and various lanterns or flashlights in handy places.

Hey, I get to use a real bathroom! I better check to make sure Sherry didn't block the pipe with rags through the rotor rooter access in the front of the house, thinking sewage could back up in the sewage system went down before I tried it though.

No garbage bag lining the bowl, must be all right I thought. So nice to have water, any kind of access to water and indoor plumbing I considered finishing up. I walked outside and rejoined the party and for once, my audience was waiting to talk to me instead of me listening to them.

"David, they say they are going to start having food distribution points next week, you think FEMA can take care of this?" Sandra asked and everyone's gaze turned in my direction.

"That's not FEMA responding most likely, although it might be." I considered. "The headquarters for the State National Guard is here in Montgomery and we have that dedicated but pitifully sized 24 man response team stationed here. They will have communications with the Governors office and the Alabama Emergency Management bunker in Clanton but since there is no plan and they got to be super short staffed, it's most likely an independent effort from one of the Guard officers." I said sipping my drink and trying to wrap my head around what really might be going on.

"What do you mean there is no Government plan? I thought

you been studying how to plan for this shit for years." Betsy said accusingly towards me.

"Hell, why do you think I prep so much? It is because I KNOW there is not a plan for something of this magnitude. At least ways nothing I have seen for civilians. They have continuity of Government plans, but those plans are for the fat cats and politicians!" I responded a bit brusquely, as it hit a nerve I had not been able to change policies in my short tenure.

I continued a bit aggressively, "While the House last year passed the "GRID Act, addressing vulnerabilities of the bulk power sector to natural threats and cyber attacks, action in the Senate is tied up by conflicting bids for jurisdiction by five different committees. So that means everyone is still talking about it and doing nothing and when they get around to it, will be slow as hell and bureaucratic B.S." I said choking from turning up my drink up too fast.

"So where is the food they're talking about coming from?" Sandra directed towards me with a shoot the messenger attitude.

"There are some pre staged supplies in warehouses here they use to pre position for Gulf disasters. This is a rally point for all the trucks that head out, remember Katrina? Maybe they are commandeering the local Winn Dixie and Piggly Wiggly warehouses, I do not know! Give me time to think on it," I said sitting back and trying to fathom the unknown, while being pelted with more questions.

"Do you know where your distribution point is yet for this address?" I said putting a hush to the babbling around me. Knowing where it was, would give me some inclination as to who was orchestrating this show.

"They said for our zip code we go to Normandale tentatively and it would be confirmed next Wednesday." Sherry said while shushing her charges and seeing my warring emotions and thoughts.

"They didn't assign colors or refer to anyone as sectors? Think back to the exact wording, it makes a difference in my understanding of things." I said slowly and clearly searching the contemplative faces around me.

155

"No, they definitely said distribution points were being assigned by zip code." Sherry said looking at me furrowing my brow and studying the meaning of what was just revealed.

"It sounds like they are using a vaccination or drug distributing plan that maps out central points for drive up delivery of medications in case of a bioterrorism attack. It will be military trucks doing the food drops; they are the only ones that can move possibly at the moment but I am still not sure who has those public health plans in their hands." I considered and wandered towards the house with Sally Cat following me and reminding me with an occasional meow that I usually gave her a treat when asked politely.

"How is the Kitty chow holding up?" I addressed Sherry from the stairs to the house.

"I am being careful, but all we got is that big sack of dry inside the door." she said worriedly.

"Ok, a few nibbles I give her won't hurt." I replied assuring the cat I would provide her something for playing tag along. I fixed a drink and gave the cat a tiny amount of kibble, and returned to my chair.

"Sandra, you and Betsy are at a disadvantage now if they are checking residency papers. But I do not foresee that as a problem at the moment. The problem is going to be this delivery is going to be a first come first served affair." I stated reminding myself of how many times I had served on Ice distribution lines while in the Guard in response to the aftermath of a hurricane.

"Its basically hand stuff off the truck to a line of people and whoever doesn't get any first go round is SOL and has to wait on another truck at another time or day. People get hostile about that, let me tell you, if they are one of the unlucky ones," I said warningly.

"This first go round, all three of you go and get there early. The house should be safe enough because most people will be going after the free distribution stuff for the first time and not studying robbing houses." I let this sink in for a moment and then carried on.

"The longer this crap lasts the people in the other zip code not

156

being served on that day, figure you're not home, so break ins start happening. If stuff is in short supply or now high valued, then robberies of people coming back from distribution points start happening. They will lay in wait for you." I said ominously, but seriously, as I had seen it before as man's inhumanity to man started to surface after a prolonged disaster.

"It won't be long before at least one of you needs to stay to guard the house while the other two go out to get what is available." I said instructing the girls to the realities of things to come.

"But, we have food David; we don't need to even get out in that danger." Sherry said while exchanging glances of apprehension with the group.

"That is a smart consideration, but not fully thought through." I cajoled not wanting to detract from the notion, but needing to get to a main point of our survival without scaring anyone too much.

"Look ladies, everyone in the neighborhood is going to be observing and talking about this possibility of getting some food distribution. You must be just as worried, just as frantic as they are that it will be successful, without letting on you have a margin of safety." I said as realizations started setting in.

"You need to be just as dirty, just as tired from walking all that way to get something to eat as everyone else to be able to not stand out, or someone will start thinking something is abnormal. Watch out for your trash you pile out on the curb, lose weight with everyone else, don't be over confident and above all else do not let on to anybody what you have been blessed with storing." I strongly advised.

"We get it David, I have been talking to everyone, already about just that, but we got neighbors and elderly here in the community that we can't just ignore." She said with a bit of venom in her voice.

"I am not saying we don't try to help them or shoot someone raiding our gardens to feed their families." I objected.

"I am merely stating the obvious and making you aware, that I do not need a target painted on the back of any one of us, if we hope to get through this." I replied a bit strongly while raising my hand to obvious dissent, but indicating I had a plan.

"This block you live on, as well as my Mom's, have to become little city states that are organized and not little neighborhood gang turfs. The structure and the organization of the communities before we had this event must be maintained and it's necessary to reestablish that normalcy now under the old guidelines that have already been accepted." I said while the rationality and plausibility of the concept became more understandable and a general acceptance of the idea was received amongst my listeners.

"Sherry, you were very active in your neighborhood association, you elected officers, interviewed representatives, had meetings with law enforcement etc. to address the problems facing your normalcy of life, did you not?" I directed my attention towards Sherry's awakening that the solution to the problem was nothing new or out of hand.

"That is correct David, the infrastructure is already in place to meet and agree to solutions to problems here in this neighborhood. How do we start to work on things, and what is the first on the agenda?" she said considering her bastion of safety no longer an island in a sea of distress.

"You call a meeting!" Betsy said surprising everyone with the most obvious solution looking nonplussed.

"See, you are all members of a committee that you did not know you were even members of." I said, looking pleased with myself, as they excitedly made plans to contact the association for further actions as I exited stage right, while picking up all the glasses to play bartender with.

"Let me interrupt your deliberations a second." I said, as I was serving drinks to my hostesses.

"Needs of those that cannot get to the distribution point and security for those that do, should be the first order of business for this meeting you propose." I said taking my own seat and the conversation resumed like I was not even there, unless a question arouse they could not agree on.

I basically ignored my friends' chatter, while I was

considering how to start up similar strategies in my Mom's neighborhood, when Sherry broke my concentration with a question.

"David, you think that ex FBI guy should be put in charge of security?" Sherry and the rest of the females tossed in my lap.

"I never met him, but he looked ok at a distance." I said refocusing and considering on how he did not look like the typical Hollywood shade wearing prick, which was my current opinion of that service.

Sherry was a bit put-off about me not thinking her idea was wonderful, and I admit I had never personally met the guy and she had, so my judgments might be biased, but I had more questions to ask before committing to the sensibilities of anything.

"You might want to consider an old military infantry man too, but I want to talk to Mr. FBI as a diplomacy effort towards the group or association I will be forming, that he might be collaborating with." Pausing long enough for everyone to see that a mutual alliance amongst different neighborhoods was part of a bigger plan to normalcy in my viewpoint.

"We need to have what is called multi agency liaisons to address all the concerns any group of people with different needs and responsibilities might face." I said, apparently complicating the matter and perplexing my would-be advocates.

'Sorry, it's a lot to think about, this is what I do. I don't manage the emergency; I coordinate at a central point a means of sharing a variety of different responses and communications.

"Dang, I always thought that you were practicing not answering a question straight, or with a question." Betsy laughed and said as she handed me another drink.

"I got to quit partaking, or you all need to quit asking so many good questions, I am afraid this day's trip has me second guessing my judgments and I am feeling a bit fuzzy." I said to obvious looks it was my fault for overindulging, but they had mercy on my poor soul.

"Oh, quit trying to carry the burden and relax, David, sometimes it is best to act very slowly before you over react."

Sherry reminded me.

"I know you're tired, David. Why don't you eat something and we won't quiz you anymore." Sherry said while patting me and visually telling her friends that now was not the time to dog pile on me for answers I did not know.

"I got to get my head clear." I said rising and stretching a bit.

"I am going to get the keys to the shed and put the tractor up and walk around front for a minute to clear the cob webs out."

Who wrote that statement that says about how I been feeling for the last few days, I believe it was Robert Frost, but all I can think of is the miles to go before I sleep.

Whose woods these are I think I know.
His house is in the village, though;
He will not see me stopping here
To watch his woods fill up with snow.

My little horse must think it queer
To stop without a farmhouse near
Between the woods and frozen lake
The darkest evening of the year.

He gives his harness bells a shake
To ask if there's some mistake.
The only other sound's the sweep
Of easy wind and downy flake.

The woods are lovely, dark and deep,
But I have promises to keep,
And miles to go before I sleep,
And miles to go before I sleep.

Daang! David you're getting pretty skippy, thinking of stuff like that versus staying in the here and now. Well 6 days of hard drinking and exercise plus the stress will do that to you. I better stay here tonight and see Mom in the morning. Sherry said she was alright and even if you did come 200 miles by country rail, the old lady would hell raise you for dabbling in the sprits.

I am just glad enough to be home and away from that hen party in the backyard for a moment, as much as I care about them. Dusk, the time the boogers and the haints come out, I was speculating on as I see moving shadows out of the corner of my eye.

Kids, teenagers actually are riding up on bikes at the far corner of the street congregating in a group of 6 or 7. Normally I would not think anything about the behavior, but they are looking about furtively like they up to something. We had a problem in the neighborhood prior to my appointment in Atlanta with break-ins and the cops told us at the association meeting it was suspected that juveniles were doing it as part of a gang initiation.

They see me watching them and I make sure to get more obvious about it by standing in the drive way and staring in their direction. I got all day and distance to win this contest, I think, leaning up against Sherry's defunct car as they lose interest and move on.

Damn kids can be more vicious than adults can be and they have not learned life's lessons yet about dire consequences, I had better add them to my list of predators to warn the girls about.

"You ok, David?" Sherry says behind me giving me a startle.

"I am ok; I was just watching and thinking." I say in an odd moment of renewed mutual affection and hugging her.

"I am staying the night, you got space somewhere?" I ask unsure of the reply, but knowing I will have the refuge I need.

"I was going to tell you, that you should consider it, we will find you a place before the night's over." she offered warmly.

"We are going to make you something special for dinner I think you might like as a homecoming meal." She said drawing my interest.

"What might that be?" I asked, filled with the joy of having some common ground to base presumptions on.

"Well, it's not Chinese takeout, but remember we bought that Mountain House Sweet and Sour Pork? I am going to add a can of shrimp to it as a treat and you can have double portions for making it home." she said with a light pat, as we looked at one of the asparagus beds that wouldn't be productive until next spring.

"That sounds absolutely wonderful!" My sprits were renewed at the prospect of Sherry tweaking all ready good food up to a culinary masterpiece and adding some special touches of spice and goodness. "I'll go clean myself up, first."

Refreshed, I returned to the kitchen and watched the roommates bustle around preparing a meal and could not help but think about how hard of times might be coming, as I saw lights and candles start to appear in the surrounding houses and nightfall started to settle on the city.

I thought I could wait to broach the subject of what I expected to happen next, but I considered time was of the essence and I needed some answers in order to safeguard my friends and family. I suppose I should have waited until after dinner to bring up the subject of possibly relocating, but the thoughts of how quickly I figured things could spin out of control made me anxious to speak.

"I am not trying to scare you all or raise any fears you must have already considered, but those food drops can't last for long and there will be an end to the service that doesn't look promising." I said looking up solemnly and throwing a wet blanket on the party

"What are you getting at David? They already started distributing food faster than you said would happen if this type of thing occurred." Sherry said with hands on hips and mad at me for spoiling the revelry with one of my doom and gloom proclamations.

"When what is stocked in Montgomery is gone, how will they get more? It used to be in this country we had enough wheat and other food to feed every man, woman and child in the US in the Strategic National Stockpile during the Cold war for 5 yrs. I don't have the statistics in front of me but the figure is something like 5 days now. We dwindled and sold off our resources to other countries. Besides, that was when trucks were

162

running." I tried to reason

"What are you saying, David?" an obviously irate Sherry demanded to know.

"I am saying, before summer ends, we should think about bugging out!" I said in exasperation to shocked looks that looked very confused.

"Look I didn't say we go tomorrow, I am just getting everyone to think about the possibilities." To stunned silence before everyone began speaking at once.

'WELL where can we go?" Sandra said above the hub bub.

"I am thinking Lake Martin. Look at this garden and we have been regularly watering." I replied waving at the now barely visible, but earlier visible memorably drooping, drought affected plants. The only thing that seemed little affected was the asparagus plants in many beds. If we go I am taking those 3yr old roots with us I mentally added to my packing list.

'We got time to discuss this later." Sherry said and got back into the groove of making a delicious dinner and ending that subject for the evening.

One good thing about dehydrated food, it was quick, add hot water wait 10 minutes and eat mostly. Sherry worked with it and polished it, but it didn't take very long and I soon had a heaping bowl of hot chow in front of me.

"This is GOOD!" I said exuberantly and Sherry commenced to explain the ingredients in her recipe, as I was starting to nod from the day's fatigue.

"You're sleeping in the computer room, I made you a bed." Betsy said returning from the house.

"I appreciate that, Thank you. I don't think I will be long for this world tonight." I yawned

"David that Xantrec 1500 power pack of yours and those 12v lights you bought is what we use for the main lighting in the living room." Sherry advised me.

"Is it working well? Have you hooked that fold up 120watt solar panel you were storing for me to it yet?"

"I haven't needed to, but I am glad you are around to show

me how to do it, if you are not going to need it yet?' she said questioning slyly if I was willing to let her keep borrowing it.

"Oh sure, hang on to it for now, its just plug and play with the charging panel, but I will check you out on it tomorrow." I replied allocating her the unit for now.

"I am going to go to sleep now. We're going to get through this." I said hugging Sherry good night.

24

SUNRISE

I awoke to a silent house and wondered what time it was because of the blacked out windows and feeble light from the one night light plugged in the Xantrec unit in the other room.

I dug my watch out and looked at the time, 5.30. I am not a morning person but I was anxious to get home.

I thought how often it was so easy if you wanted coffee you just cut the stove on. Well that is not happening here, Sherry had an electric range.

I went to Sherrie's bedroom and called softly to her, "Sherry, Sherry…"

"Hey, David, what time is it?" She replied not bothering to open her eyes.

"Its early, I am taking off." I said just wishing to say good bye.

"Hang on I will get up, let's have coffee before you go." she said starting to sit up.

"Ok, I will wait on you in the backyard and get the stove going." I replied moving in that direction.

"Just use the little propane stove to heat some water, it's a special occasion." she said smiling and becoming fully awake. "I will get it in a minute; you don't know where everything's at."

Sherry put purified water in a small kettle and got the propane canister stove going and motioned me out the back door.

"David after you went to bed last night I had a talk with Betsy and Sandra. They said 'We go when you say', David, but are you sure we have to go?"

"Eventually I think we will, but no rush, I just got back and I really don't know the lay of the land here yet." I said looking at the garden and really not knowing anything this early in the morning.

"We got to be sure we do the right thing David." she said while greeting the cat who had wandered up.

"I know its going to be hard decision." I said commiserating with her.

"Let's have that coffee and enjoy the sunrise." I said putting the worries behind us for now.

"Lets do." and she turned to go get it.

Sherry returned with our coffees and we settled down in front of the outdoor table to wake up a bit and talk a bit.

"Anything we should be doing David, besides what I have already done?" she said studying my response.

"No, you're doing fine, I would suggest though you distribute whatever bug out gear extras you got between Betsy and Sandra, so they got their own bags.

"We are working on that, there's just been so much going on and to do." she said sadly.

"You're doing great; you know it might be a few days before I can get back over."

"See if those little 15 mile radios you got at the house still work and bring one back with you when you come if they do." she advised me and bringing back a memory of what I hoped was 30 bucks well spent at Wal-Mart years ago.

"The batteries are not in them, so it's possible I can get them going." I responded wishing for a less technical subject this morning, but understanding the very important implications of it.

"Be sure that Betsy and Sandra know how to get to my Mom's house in case they need to." I said thinking about contingencies.

"Your house is closer to the food distribution point than mine, so that is a good idea." she said sipping her coffee and both of us dreading the next goodbye, no matter how short.

"I need to sneak in and get your bike out of the living room." I told her while considering anything else needing to be said before I left.

"You locked the garage well last night?" Sherry asked.

Ah hell the tractor! Maybe I ought to leave directions to crank that old booger.

"I need a piece of paper and a pen in case you need to ever crank that tractor, if I am not here." I said rising and heading towards the house.

"Oh, I could figure it out." Sherry began confidently.

"Believe me, you couldn't and I don't want you getting hurt trying. I will write it down." I said and did. Before leaving, we shared a warm and prolonged embrace and I promised to return as soon as I could.

I mounted the bicycle and waved good bye for now to Sherry and peddled swiftly towards home. This was a girl's bike, but at least it was a respectable looking mountain bike I mused.

The neighborhoods were pretty quite at this early hour and I didn't see anyone about. I wheeled up in the driveway and sure enough like she had done every morning of her life the curtains were drawn to let in the morning Sun.

I glimpsed her hurrying to the door from the window and rushed to meet her.

The door opened and we didn't even take time to say anything as we hugged one another. *Home, home at last, now we see what the day will bring.* I thought looking down on my happily question gushing Mom.

The End

BOOK (1) of the Prepper Trilogy

My Readers Might Also Enjoy:

THE RURAL RANGER A SUBURBAN AND URBAN SURVIVAL MANUAL & FIELD GUIDE OF TRAPS AND SNARES FOR FOOD AND SURVIVAL
By Ron Foster

The Modern Day Survival Primer for Solving Modern Day Survival Problems! This book will teach you the techniques to not just survive, but to use ingenuity and household items to solve your problems scientifically with a bit of primitive know how thrown in. A complete and detailed section utilizing explicit drawings and easy to understand photographs covers thoroughly the topic of survival trapping using Modern Snares, Deadfalls, Conibear Traps, and Primitive Snares. This book is dedicated for long term survival in the country or the suburbs to insure you survive and thrive! Build a solar oven or pasteurize water its all in here! Catch your dinner, then cook it or preserve it too! Food procurement is the name of the game along with purified water in a survival or disaster situation. Are you ready?

Made in the USA
Charleston, SC
03 September 2013